SABOTAGE

A novel

JEFF GOMEZ

Harrow Books

For the three wise men

There is nothing more important to a patrol officer than the partner with whom he will share more waking hours than with a wife, upon whom he is to depend more than a man should, with whom he will share the ugliness and tedium, the humor and the wonder.

—JOSEPH WAMBAUGH
THE ONION FIELD

ACT

I

THE DONUT SHOP on Pico and Fairfax had always been the Chief's favorite. He went there almost every day, either on his way into the station—picking up a few dozen for the boys rolling off patrol and the detectives about to start their day—or else on the way home so he could munch on a maple bar as he fought the traffic back to San Pedro. Today, he and his new partner were eating their breakfast in the parking lot from a white paper bag placed on the trunk of their plain wrapped 1976 Plymouth. Because this was only his second week as a detective, everyone's been calling Bobby the Rookie. The Chief thought it'd be good to take Bobby out for donuts on the day of his first big bust.

"Chief, these donuts are amazing."

Born Oscar Martinez, everyone called him the Chief because he'd been on the force for so long. He went through the academy in the early sixties and was just a few years shy of pulling the pin. Also, his head of gray hair made him look older than he was. Not that he minded. The Chief loved being the guy everyone in the department turned to for advice.

"Stick with me, Bobby." The Chief took a big bite out of a donut, purple jelly dribbling down his chin until he lapped it up with his tongue. "I'll show you things."

"Yeah, but we didn't even pay for them."

The Chief had made a half-hearted attempt, beginning to reach for his wallet after asking for the half dozen, but the owner—a large guy with thick glasses named Tadlock—just smiled and waved him off.

"You must have had your eating spots when you were in uniform."

"Sure," said the Rookie. "I never paid for a meal when I was on patrol. But I figured all that would change once I was pulling my duty in plainclothes."

There were plenty of places around LA where cops out of uniform could eat for free, if not half price. Either the owners knew you from your beat, or else they figured you for a detective by the way you dressed. And if that didn't work, a cop could just flash his badge or gun while going for his wallet.

"Tadlock's an ex-boxer," the Chief explained, pointing to the donut shop with his nearly empty cup of coffee. "They used to call him 'Instant Death.' Had a right hook that would just lay guys out cold. He made some noise on the circuit up north, but when he came down here for some bigger bouts, he got clobbered. He's put on a few pounds since then, and his eyes are gone, so now he runs this joint. We park out here where everyone can see us, and he's happy. He doesn't get robbed, and we get free donuts and coffee."

Just then Tadlock came out with two more Styrofoam cups, steam coming off the black liquid. When he approached, Tadlock cast a shadow over the two detectives. His eyes, seen through the thick frames, were large and blurry.

"Figured you guys could use another round."

Taking one of the cups, the Chief said, "Thanks, Tadlock. You're the best."

The Rookie took his wordlessly, waiting until the owner was back inside to speak again. "I don't know why he's worried about getting robbed. Who'd pull a gun on him? He's huge."

The Chief just shrugged as he chewed.

Bobby finished up a powdered donut and asked, "So, what's the bust today, Chief?"

They'd only been partners a week, and it'd been pretty quiet. Things usually heated up in the summer. Tourists came into town and made easy victims, and college kids poured onto the beaches for three months of surfing and buying pot or pills. It usually added up to action. But not this year. It was already mid-June and they hadn't managed a pinch since Bobby got promoted to detective at the first of the month. The Rookie couldn't wait to make his first real bust.

"A guy's in from South Africa to make a buy. Heroin," said the Chief. "Name's Wallace. British. A high-class dude, which is why we call him *Sir* Stewart Wallace, as a joke."

"He been picked up before?"

The Chief nodded. "Up to now, we've only managed to pin small stuff on him. Little amounts here and there. But he's not who we're after. I want to find out who his source is. Where he's getting the stuff."

The Rookie reached into the bag for another donut.

"How are we going to do that?"

The Chief waved his own half-eaten donut in the air as he spoke. He'd only taken a few bites out of it.

"An informant gave me a tip last week. Said the deal's going down this morning at a motel in Atwater Village. We're going stop it before it happens. That should lead us to whoever Wallace is getting the stuff from."

"How do you know it's a good tip? This CI give you good information in the past?"

The Chief looked around slyly, as if he didn't want anyone to overhear what he was about to say. But they were the only ones in the parking lot. Inside the donut shop, Tadlock was talking to two guys from LAPD in uniform. Muffled laughter could be heard all the way to where the Chief and the Rookie were standing.

"It's not exactly a registered confidential informant, okay? He's a guy I've been running off book."

The Rookie whistled, impressed. "How'd you get that to fly with the lieutenant?"

Now it was the Chief's turn to grin. "Hey, what the lieutenant doesn't know won't hurt him." The Chief relaxed a bit, adding, "Look, if I bring in a solid bust, the lieutenant's not going to care where I'm getting my information."

"That's why they call you the Chief."

As the Rookie took another big bite, the Chief turned and looked at the sun. It was already eighty degrees. The mountains and the smog seemed to trap the heat over Los Angeles, and all the concrete and cars didn't help. The freeways were ovens, the crowded streets of Hollywood factories that generated heat.

The Rookie was wearing a short-sleeved white shirt with two breast pockets and red stripes, ironed crisp, along with a tie. His pants were brown polyester slacks, straight from Sears. But the Chief was wearing a gray trench coat over a dark blue suit, along with a white shirt and tie. They both had sunglasses on, the Chief's silver, the Rookie's dark brown. In California, you wore them all day long. For the Rookie, who was raised on the East Coast, this was paradise. For the Chief, who'd lived in Southern California all his life, it was just another day.

"Jesus, it's hot," the Chief said.

"Why're you wearing that coat?" The Rookie laughed. "It's going to be ninety degrees today. Don't you watch the news?"

"I live down near the water." The Chief talked as he took off the coat. "When I got up this morning, it was foggy and cold."

He lifted the bag of donuts so he could open the trunk of the Plymouth. Inside, he saw the standard gear: shotgun, shells, megaphone, handcuffs. He tossed in the jacket.

When he closed the trunk, he discovered someone new standing next to the car. The Chief jumped a little.

"Cochese, Jesus, you scared me." But then the Chief relaxed again, taking a sip of his coffee. "What brings you here?"

Before he could answer, the Rookie—his face full of glazed donut—said, "Have a donut. We got a bunch."

Cochese was wearing shades, as well as a tie and a short-sleeve shirt. His black hair was worn longer than the Chief's or even the Rookie's. The lieutenant didn't like it, but as a detective, Cochese could get away with it. The bluecoats on patrol looked like they were from the sixties, with their hair short on the sides and back—some of them had flattops, as if Parker was still in charge—but Cochese definitely looked the part of 1978. He'd fit in at any disco in town.

Cochese shook off the offer of food and addressed the Chief. "I'm looking for you, not donuts."

Cochese was from the South and, occasionally, he sounded like it. But rather than stand out, his slow drawl blended right in with the casual pace of California.

"Me?" The Chief sounded surprised. "What for?"

"Shadrach's gone missing."

Roy Shadrach, Cochese's partner, had been the Chief's partner years ago.

"What's old Roy gone and done now?"

"This isn't a joke, Chief. He hasn't been heard from in two days."

As the Chief thought about this, the Rookie reached into the bag for yet another donut. He ate half of it in one bite.

"Maybe he's just working on a case you don't know about," suggested the Chief.

"Could be, I don't know," replied Cochese, pacing. "I found his service revolver in a filing cabinet, so wherever he was going, he wasn't expecting any heat."

"Well then, there you go," said the Chief. "He's off somewhere bowling for dollars."

When Cochese didn't laugh at the joke, the Chief turned serious and added, "What's the watch commander say about it?"

Cochese stuck his hands in his pockets and kicked at the gravelly parking lot.

"I haven't told him yet. I'm trying to protect Roy."

"From what?" asked the Chief.

"I don't know," answered Cochese. "Last week some case he'd been working on got cold, so Shadrach said he was going to kill some time with something else. Said he had a favor to fulfill, or a lead, or something. He didn't tell me what it was."

"When was that?"

The detective looked up at the hazy California sky, trying to remember.

"Friday."

"Shit, Cochese," snapped the Chief. "So all you're telling me is that he didn't show up to work today? That's nothing to get upset about. He probably just had some plans from the weekend that spilled into today."

"No, no." Cochese shook his head back and forth. "On Friday I asked him what he was going do during the weekend. Like, was it his weekend with the kids or what."

Shadrach, like a lot of cops—including the Chief—was divorced. His had been particularly ugly, with accusations of infidelity dragged into court and Roy getting stuck having to pay a huge amount of alimony and child support.

"And what'd he say?" asked the Chief.

As Cochese tried to remember the exact answer, the Rookie stuck his hand into the bag for the last donut.

"He said he had to check out something that wasn't

work related. He had to, I can't remember exactly what phrase he used. Something like, 'talk to someone' or 'go find somebody.'"

The Chief let out a laugh. "Jesus, Cochese, the guy's probably just trying to get laid." He finally finished the donut he'd been holding in his hand ever since Cochese approached him and the Rookie. As he chewed, he said, "Give the guy a break. He was feeling lonely and wanted to meet someone. Maybe he didn't and it made him so sad he went on a bender that he's still out somewhere sleeping off. Or maybe he scored with some broad, and they're in bed right now having a grand old time."

Cochese didn't buy any of it. "No, Chief, that doesn't fit. Shadrach laid off the sauce years ago, and even if he'd met some chick, why wouldn't he come in? Or leave me a message or something?"

The Chief just waved away Cochese's questions and finished chewing. The white bag on the trunk of the Plymouth was now empty. The Chief looked at his watch. It was still early, not even ten. Wallace was set to make the buy at eleven.

"Look, Cochese," said the Chief, "you want to make yourself useful today? Me and the Rookie here have got a nice bust and we could use some backup."

Cochese asked, "What's the blueprint?"

As the Chief laid out the operation, Cochese just nodded.

"Sounds like a solid bust, I'm in."

"Good. Let's head back to the station so we can ditch one of our cars. It'll be easier just taking one."

Cochese headed for his car. The Rookie, hopped up on sugar, could hardly contain himself.

"Come on, Chief. I'm ready for Wallace."

The Chief grinned and grabbed the empty bag from the top of the trunk. As he crumpled it, he said, "Let's go get him."

THE CHIEF LET the Rookie drive back to the station. Their Plymouth may have been unmarked, but everything about it screamed COP CAR. It was too plain, too boring, too ugly to be anything else. The glove box held their radio and a red light that attached to the roof for pursuits.

"This is a good way for you to get to know the area," said the Chief. "After another week behind the wheel, you'll know Wilshire Division as well as you knew Hollenbeck."

The Rookie shuddered. "God, I hope not. Just thinking of Boyle Heights makes my stomach hurt."

"I bet," said the Chief as they rolled through the neighborhood. Streets were wide, houses were Spanish, palm trees lined the sidewalks. "It's a different world up here."

The Rookie turned onto Pickford and then Spaulding. Stuck behind a light, the Chief said, "Bobby, are you sure you know where you're going? These are goddamn surface streets."

The Rookie's smile disappeared for a second. "Sure," he said, adding, "I can just *feel* my way."

And with that, the cocky grin returned. The light turned green and the Rookie continued winding through the residential area as the Chief just shook his head. He knew that there'd be a day, or an incident, that would wipe that smile right off the Rookie's face. It might be in two months, or two years, but something would happen—a killer going free, or an innocent man going to jail—and that grin of the Rookie's would be gone for good. On that day, he'd no longer be the Rookie.

"Jesus Christ," exclaimed Bobby, his hands gripping the wheel. "Take a look at *that*."

The Chief saw a woman in a housecoat standing on the sidewalk, trying to flag them down.

"What do we do?" The Rookie looked from the woman to his partner. "Do we stop, or what?"

The Chief sat up straight. "Goddamnit, Bobby, just keep going. Cochese is waiting. We've got a bust today."

But the Rookie couldn't kill his old habits. Out of instinct, his two years in the patrol car coming back to him, he pulled over near where the woman had finally stopped hopping up and down. The Rookie killed the engine and then looked sheepishly at the Chief. "Sorry."

"For chrissakes," fumed the Chief, "we don't have time for this."

"Let's just see what she wants, okay?"

The Chief muttered something under his breath and reluctantly got out of the car. Bobby joined him at the curb. The woman, finally seeing them outside the Plymouth, took a step back.

"Oh," she said, sounding disappointed. "You're not who I thought you were."

The Rookie replied, "Ma'am?"

"I wanted the police, it's—I was expecting the police." She pointed at the Plymouth. "I saw your car and just thought—"

The Chief cut her off. "Look, lady, do you need help? Are you in danger in some way?"

The woman put her hands into the pockets of her housecoat.

"It's my—my daughter. She—she's missing." The woman spoke in halting sentences, her eyes darting from side to side.

"Missing?" The Rookie pulled a small notebook and pen out of his back pocket and began writing.

This made the Chief groan. He leaned over and whispered to the Rookie, "Bobby, don't get involved."

Not waiting to be asked anything else, the woman continued.

"Her name's Dellie. She's seventeen and hasn't been home in a week. I'm just so sick, I don't know what to do."

The Rookie stopped writing long enough to ask, "Have you filed a missing persons report?"

The woman looked confused. Her eyebrows knitted into question marks.

"Well, I'm—I don't know. I spoke to *someone*, I know that. I thought you were him."

The Rookie was about to say something when the Chief stepped forward.

"We'll check with the station and see if there's been any movement, okay? In the meantime, we're very late for another appointment. Thank you, and have a nice day."

The Chief was turning to leave when the woman said, "Wait." She pulled from a pocket a photograph. When she spoke again, her voice was choked by emotion. She said, "My daughter, Dellie."

The photo was snatched out of her hand by the Chief. He got into the car and slammed the door. From inside the Plymouth, he growled, "Bobby, let's *go.*"

The Rookie shook the woman's hand, quickly apologized for his partner's behavior, and then joined the Chief in the car. As they drove away, he said, "You didn't need to be so hard on her. Her daughter's missing."

The Chief grunted. "Daughter? She's just a foster parent, Bobby. Probably worried more about the monthly check than the girl."

The Rookie finally turned onto Venice. The station was just a few blocks away. Stopped at a red light at Mansfield, he looked at the picture the woman had given them. The girl was young and thin, her light brown hair feathered and parted in the middle.

"Quit a looker," Bobby said.

The Chief just ignored him.

Pulling into the station, they saw Cochese leaning against his car and chewing a toothpick. His black hair blew in the warm breeze.

"Jesus, guys," he said, walking with the car as Bobby pulled up alongside Cochese's cruiser, an even older version of what the Rookie was driving. "Where have you been?"

"The Rookie here wanted to make an unexpected stop." The Chief got out of the car. "Any sign of Shadrach?"

Cochese shook his head.

"Then it looks like you're still with us for the day. Okay if we take your car?"

Cochese nodded and got behind the wheel. The Chief took the front seat.

"Rookie," he said, "you're in the back."

THE MOTEL ROOM stank of beer and urine. A queen bed sagged in the center, as if it'd given up a long time ago, while the Magic Finger machine attached to the headboard had a hand-written note that read OUT OF ORDER. The sign out front advertised color TVs—the word COLOR lit up like a rainbow in neon—but all this room had was an old black-and-white that had seen better days. Not that anyone would complain. People who stayed at the Hello Nasty either brought their entertainment with them, or didn't hang around long enough to be bored.

"Where'd you get these disguises, Chief? My pants are huge."

The Chief looked and saw the Rookie putting on a bellboy's uniform that was at least two sizes too large. The Chief, meanwhile, was putting on a white chef's jacket.

"Just do the best you can."

The Rookie grumbled as he put on the last part of the uniform, a round hat that made him feel like a fool. The Chief just laughed, and then put on the chef's hat. This made the Rookie laugh.

"See? We're even," the Chief said. "We both look like idiots."

A set of walkie-talkies on the table suddenly crackled to life, Cochese's voice coming in loud and clear

"Guys, I'm in position."

The Chief barked at the Rookie. "Turn those down,

for chrissakes. You want to let the whole motel know we're here?"

The Rookie scrambled to the table and turned down the volume on each of the walkie-talkies. He then handed one to the Chief.

"Cochese, we just got dressed. We'll head out and begin to patrol the area in just a minute. Any sign of Wallace?"

They'd parked down the block, Cochese staying with the car so he could get a good look at whoever approached the motel. The Chief and the Rookie had entered through a side gate and quietly entered room 205, which the Chief had rented the day before so he could stash the disguises.

"No sign yet," Cochese announced through the walkie-talkie. "No one's come in or out since we got here."

The Chief looked at his watch: 10:42.

"Sounds good. Wallace is due in about fifteen minutes, so keep your eyes peeled and your ears open. He'll be carrying a load of cash, but stay out of sight until he makes the buy. I want to get his supplier. We'll radio if we need any backup; otherwise keep the line clear because we're taking our walkie-talkies with us."

"Got it, and good luck."

The walkie-talkies gave a final crackle before there was silence again in the room.

"Okay," the Chief said, "you know what you're supposed to do?"

The Rookie pointed to a silver tray filled with dishes, silverware, and glasses the Chief had brought from home.

"I'm just going to patrol the area, holding the tray. If anyone asks, I'm a bellboy delivering room service."

"Good. And you saw the mug shots of Wallace from those prior arrests, so you know what he looks like."

The Rookie nodded, so the Chief continued. "And I'm a chef on my way to get more supplies for the kitchen."

The Rookie nodded again, but then thought of something. "Chief, this is a hot sheet motel. They don't have room service *or* bellboys. What if the manager sees us and tells us to get lost?"

Now it was the Chief's turn to grin. "Don't worry about that, Bobby. I laid an extra fifty on him yesterday so he wouldn't give us any trouble. He'll have his eyes closed the whole morning."

"That's smart, Chief."

The Chief tapped his temple with the index finger of his left hand. "It's all up here, Bobby. Just use your head and you'll be okay."

The Rookie slipped one of the walkie-talkies inside his absurdly large double-breasted coat. He picked up the tray, gave a final nod to the Chief, and exited the room. The Chief grabbed the remaining walkie-talkie and left room 205, heading the opposite direction of the Rookie. For the next half hour, they walked up and down the halls and perimeter of the motel. Checkout time had passed and check-in wasn't for another couple of hours, so no one was around. It was as quiet as a graveyard.

On the south balcony, the Chief and the Rookie passed each other.

"Something's wrong," whispered the Rookie. "He should be here by now."

But the Chief was calm. He just tapped his temple again and said, "Use your head, Bobby. Just keep calm and use your head."

The Rookie nodded, took a deep breath, and they again went their separate ways. Twenty minutes later, the Chief radioed.

"Bobby, you see anything out of the ordinary?"

The Rookie was on the second story of the motel, having just finished a sweep of the first floor. Down the hall was the room they were using as their base. He slipped out the walkie-talkie and answered as quietly as he could.

"Nothing from my end."

Cochese didn't have to be asked to contribute.

"Same out here, guys. Plenty of people have driven by, but no one's stopped or gotten out."

"Goddamn," the Chief said. "Maybe we missed him. Cochese, we'll head back to the room to change, and then we'll come meet you to head back to the station."

Bobby was about to slip the walkie-talkie back into his coat when he saw someone coming out of room 216. The guy was tall and skinny, wearing a tan suit and carrying a black briefcase. He had blond hair and a mustache.

The Rookie flashed back to the mug shots. A jolt of adrenaline shot through his body as he realized it was Wallace. He instantly bolted, the tray of dishes flying out of his hand as he began to run. As everything crashed to the ground, Wallace looked and saw Bobby barreling toward him, his hat flying off and falling over the railing. It took Wallace less than a second to react and take off.

"Wallace is here! Repeat, Wallace is *here*," the Rookie shouted into his walkie-talkie as Wallace disappeared around a corner. "Am pursuing on foot."

The Chief shouted back, followed by something from Cochese, but the Rookie didn't hear. His heart was pounding so hard he could feel it pulse through his entire body. Finally reaching the corner, he was at the top of the steps leading to the first floor. Wallace was already halfway down the stairs. The Rookie took two steps at a time, trying to catch up, his baggy pants not making it easy to run.

At the bottom he had a choice between a sidewalk that led to the front of the motel and another that led to the back way he'd come with the Chief an hour before. He knew Cochese had the front staked out, so the Rookie bolted through the opening behind the motel. He was just in time to see Wallace dart around a sign that said SWIM AT YOUR OWN RISK: NO LIFEGUARD ON DUTY.

The Rookie sprinted and caught up to Wallace just as he got to the edge of the motel's small pool. Through a space in a chain-link fence that led to an alley, the Rookie could see a gray Dodge Charger. Its engine was on, the rough idling ricocheting between the buildings. Wallace's getaway car. The Rookie knew this was his only chance.

Wallace stopped for a second and looked back. Just as he turned, Bobby leaped into the air and grabbed Wallace, sending them both into the pool. Wallace lost his grip of the briefcase as he slammed into the water. When they came up for air, breathing heavily, the briefcase was floating toward the corner like a raft on a wave. The Charger in the alley sped away. The Rookie grinned.

"Sorry, Wallace. It looks like you just missed your ride." He reached into his baggy pants for a pair of handcuffs. As he put one of the steel rings around Wallace's thin wrist, Bobby said with a smirk, "Don't worry. We'll give you a lift."

BACK AT THE station, the three detectives tried to figure out how they'd missed the bust.

"No one came or went out of the front of the motel,"

Cochese said as they were sitting around a desk in the detectives' room. There were four desks in the large room, but the other three were empty since it was lunchtime and everyone was either out on cases or out getting food. On the desk was Wallace's open briefcase. It held a bit of cash and eleven Saran-wrapped bricks of heroin The Chief was sitting behind the desk, while the Rookie and Cochese were seated at metal chairs in front of it.

"And we were patrolling the halls." The Rookie looked first at Cochese, and then at the Chief. "Nothing happened until Wallace came out of the room and made a run for it."

The Chief considered this. "That means the deal must have gone down *before* we got there. Not after."

"And Wallace was just sitting tight," replied the Rookie, "waiting until the coast was clear to make his escape."

The three of them shook their heads, trying to put the facts in order and come up with a theory about what had happened.

The Rookie pointed at the briefcase. There had originally been a dozen bricks of heroin, but one of the bricks had been sent to the lab for testing, in case they could match it to junk that came up in future busts and connect it to Wallace.

"We got the drugs," he said. "That's good, right?"

The Chief shrugged. "Wallace was going to get on a plane with this stuff. I wanted his contact *here*."

"Maybe he'll give up a name in order to get a better deal." The Rookie pointed again at the briefcase. "Possession with intent. He'll never see daylight again unless he plays ball."

The Chief kicked at the leg of the metal desk. It weighed as much as his Corolla. It didn't move an inch.

"Wallace is *already* back on the street, Bobby. He made bail. His lawyer was here waiting for him." The Chief took his badge out of the interior pocket of the blue suit and threw it on the desk. "With that high-powered attorney of his, we'd be lucky to send him to county for six months, let alone San Quentin."

Cochese, who'd been staring intently at the briefcase, finally spoke. "Say that again."

"We'd be lucky to send him to county."

"No, the part about his attorney."

"His lawyer," the Chief repeated. "Some slimeball from the Valley. He was here waiting for Wallace."

Cochese leaned forward, putting his elbows on the desk. "But Wallace hadn't even been booked yet. Hadn't made a phone call. How did he know?"

"How did *who* know?" asked the Rookie.

"Wallace's lawyer," Cochese answered. "If Wallace wasn't here yet to make the call, then someone must have called *for* him."

"The Dodge," said the Rookie. "The guy in the get-away car."

The Chief and Cochese both nodded.

"That solves that," said the Chief. "The guy in the gray Charger let the big boss know that Wallace had been pinched. The big boss then reached out to the lawyer. But what about the rest of it?"

"The rest of what?" asked the Rookie.

Cochese looked at the Chief. "How well do you trust your informant?"

"He's never let me down yet."

Cochese slipped a toothpick out of his breast pocket, stripped off the paper wrapping, and placed it in the corner of his mouth. Chewing, he said, "There's a first time for everything."

Still searching for answers, the Rookie asked, "What about the hotel manager? Did he see anything?"

The Chief grumbled. "Remember when I told you he'd keep his eyes shut? Well, he did. When I asked who paid for room 216, he just said, 'My customers all look alike.' Maybe if we leaned on him a little, we could get more out of him, but I don't think there's much there."

Cochese stood up and paced around the room. "I don't like this," he said.

"What?" asked the Rookie.

"It feels like we're being set up. Sabotaged. The bad

bust, Wallace's lawyer here waiting for him, and still no Shadrach."

"Don't forget the girl."

The Chief shot the Rookie a look as Cochese stopped pacing.

"What girl?"

"Some crazy broad flagged us down," said the Chief nonchalantly. "It's nothing."

The Rookie reached into his pocket and produced the photo the old woman had given him that morning. Cochese leaned over and grabbed it.

"Quite a looker," he said. "Who is she?"

The Chief snatched the photo out of Cochese's hand and placed it facedown on the desk.

"Forget about her," he said. "Let's stay focused on Wallace."

The Rookie leaned forward and poked at the briefcase.

"If Wallace is gone, then this is all we have."

The three detectives stood and examined the briefcase. It was a standard black Samsonite with two silver latches and a plastic handle. The Chief had seen hundreds. Filled with counterfeit money, pornographic photos, forged documents. This one looked like all the others.

"There," said the Rookie, pointing to the seam near one of the hinges. "The lining."

The Chief bent over to examine it more closely. Part of

the black felt had come undone. The Chief poked around with his finger. The fabric was loose, like it'd been removed and re-glued. He grabbed as much as he could of the material and pulled. A length of lining came away in a long strip. Cochese grabbed it out of the Chief's hand to get a look. He grinned. Turning it over, he showed the Chief and the Rookie. Written in blue ink was the name *Jimmy James*.

"Bingo," said the Chief.

"The Egg Man," said Cochese.

The Rookie looked puzzled. "Who's the Egg Man? Or Jimmy James?"

The Chief stepped out from behind the desk and said, "They're the same person. Let's go pay them both a visit."

Jimmy James was a low-level hood everyone in Wilshire Division had run into at one time or another. Money laundering, prostitution, stealing cars, James did it all. But he was also smart. Despite all the arrests and charges over the years, the DA had never made anything more than a misdemeanor stick. The most time he'd done was three months a few years ago at an honor farm up in Ojai. James came back tanned, rested, and ready to continue breaking the law.

He lived in a cheap apartment complex called the

Shambala just south of Beverly. He loved to eat, so when the three detectives didn't find him at his apartment, they went to Farmers Market, a collection of restaurants and food stalls just a few blocks away. They figured he'd either be out for lunch or stocking up on supplies for his next meal. In fact, he got his nickname because, a few years ago when some bluecoats raided the Shambala on a tip about stolen guns, they'd broken into James's apartment only to find him calmly eating a plate of scrambled eggs. When the officers, with guns drawn, barked at James to get on the floor with his hands behind his head, he calmly replied that he'd comply as soon as he finished his eggs. Ever since, he's been known around town as the Egg Man.

Now, as the detectives scanned the crowd at Farmers Market, weary eyes avoided their glances. The petty criminals—shoplifters and pickpockets—instantly made them as cops and decided to knock off early for the day, or else try their luck up at Grauman's.

The Chief had described the Egg Man to the Rookie as being five eight, with long sideburns and a big belly.

For an hour the trio searched the stores, vendors, and lunch counters. Cochese was also looking for his partner. They'd checked again at the station after getting back from the Wallace bust, seeing if Shadrach had called in or, better yet, suddenly appeared. Cochese had half-expected to see Roy sitting at their usual spot in the detectives' room, smiling and giving him a hard time for palling around with the Chief and the Rookie all morning. When he wasn't at the station, Cochese had called Shadrach's house again. No answer.

"There, there," said the Rookie, trying to keep his voice down. He was pointing at someone in the crowd. "Is that the Egg Man?"

The Chief stopped and looked, but it wasn't James.

"Jesus, Bobby, Jimmy's not *that* fat. Keep looking."

After circling inside Farmers Market twice, they decided to walk around the outer edge, first along the border at West Third Street and then behind the shops. At the northeast corner, where you could see Television City just beyond a parking lot, Jimmy James rounded the corner. His gut was hanging out of a patterned blue suit, and in each arm was a bag full of groceries. The Chief and Cochese jogged to where he was and stood in front of him, while the Rookie quickly sidled up behind.

"Jimmy James," said the Chief. "What do you say we take a ride? We'd like to ask you some questions."

The Egg Man's eyes slyly shifted left and right, looking for an escape route. Finally, his arms relaxed and he let out a breath; he knew he wasn't going anywhere.

Jimmy James let the groceries fall to the ground and, with a grunt, allowed the Chief to lead him to where Cochese's Plymouth was parked around the corner. When the Rookie looked back, he saw a stain on the bottom of one of the bags. Broken eggs were seeping onto the hot pavement.

THE CHIEF'S FAVORITE interrogation room was at the end of the hall on the fifth floor, the last of four identical rooms. The other three of which were currently empty. The Chief liked this one because, if things got out of hand, the officer stationed at the end of the hall-way—who was responsible for signing in and out the rooms and writing down who was being interro-gated—wasn't likely to hear anything.

Right now, there wasn't much to hear. They'd been grilling Jimmy James for an hour about Wallace, the drugs, and being the getaway for the bust that morning, but James wasn't saying much. He insisted he'd been at home all morning until going out to get some groceries. In response to every question, threat, or accusation, he repeated the same story and ended up with the same god-damn smile on his face. The Chief thought that bringing him to the station might make him talk—impressing upon him the gravity of the situation—but James was too cool for that.

"Look," the Chief finally said, exhausted, "we found your name on Wallace." He pointed to the briefcase they'd picked up at the bust earlier in the day. "That proves you're working together."

"That don't prove a damn thing, and you know it," the Egg Man said through his grin.

"Well then, how did it get there?" asked Cochese, his voice rising.

"What can I say," laughed the Egg Man, "I'm a popular guy."

The Rookie, who'd just been sitting in the corner, letting Cochese and the Chief do the talking, suddenly snapped. He jumped out of the metal chair and attacked Jimmy James from behind, raining down blows with his right hand. Cochese jumped aside as the Egg Man did his best to protect himself with his arms. After half a dozen punches, the Chief broke in and separated the two.

As the Rookie was pushed into the hallway by his partner, the grin on Jimmy James's face disappeared for the first time.

"Bobby, Bobby," the Chief said, his voice low but serious. Behind them, in the interrogation room, they could hear Cochese continuing to ask questions. "For chrissakes, you gotta calm down or he'll sue the entire department."

The Rookie bobbed up and down, his fists still clenched, adrenaline rushing through his body.

"Sorry, Chief. It's just, I'm like Buddy Rich when I fly off the handle."

"I know, Bobby, I know. But remember, you're not in uniform busting a couple of kids for having a five-inch blade, okay? The Egg Man could give us the big supplier."

The Rookie continued to seethe, pacing up and down the hallway.

"Then what's our next move, Chief? He's playing us for suckers."

The Chief tapped his temple. "I've got an idea. I know a guy at the Department of Motor Vehicles. I'll give him a call."

"What for?"

"I want to see what the Egg Man is driving these days."

The Rookie and the Chief reentered the room, finding it very much the way they left it, except the Egg Man's grin was even bigger than before.

"Anything new?" asked the Chief.

"If he knows anything," replied Cochese, "he ain't talking."

The Chief just stood there. After a minute, he said, "Okay, Jimmy, stand up. I think we're done here."

The Egg Man got up, and the Chief and the Rookie stepped aside to let him go by. Cochese remained standing in the corner, glowering over the open briefcase. As James began to exit the room, the Chief said, "Jimmy, this is your last chance. Who sold Wallace the drugs?"

With the same grin on his face, he replied, "Gee, I forget."

"In that case, put him in the lockup for the night." The Chief nodded at the Rookie. "Maybe that'll jog his memory."

The Egg Man finally turned serious. "You can't hold me overnight! What's the charge?"

As the Rookie began to escort Jimmy James down to the cells, the Chief called after them, "We'll think of something."

THE BROUHAHA WAS a cop hangout located just north of Santa Monica Boulevard on Las Palmas. Day and night, the parking lot was filled with police cruisers and unmarked cop cars. At the bar, discussions ranged from boasting to bitching, either taking credit for a collar or complaining about some new departmental rule they were all supposed to follow. It was a place where on- or off-duty cops could drink, eat, and be with their own kind.

"So your friend at the DMV is sure," said Cochese.

The three detectives were in a corner booth, sipping on beers and going over the day's events.

The Chief took a sip and nodded. "Yup," he said. "Nineteen seventy-four Dodge Charger, registered to one Jameson James. Dark gray."

"The car I saw at the Hello Nasty," replied the Rookie.

All three detectives nodded.

"Okay, then," said Cochese, "things are adding up. Wallace was in town to make a score, and the Egg Man was his driver."

"Yeah," scoffed the Chief, "except we're missing the main ingredient. The source. Without that, all we have are two cheap busts on dirtbags we already had on our radar."

They all took another sip. Elton John's "Bennie and the Jets" was playing on the jukebox.

"And no Roy," added Cochese.

"Will you forget about that? I tell you, he's okay. Hell"—the Chief nodded toward the crowd—"he may even be here."

Cochese scanned the room. He saw plenty of familiar faces, but none of them belonged to his partner.

Netty, the club's only waitress, cut through the throng of cops and dropped off a basket of onion rings. It was now almost five o'clock, and the detectives hadn't eaten anything since the donut shop that morning. This would be their lunch and, depending on what happened next, their dinner.

Cochese and the Rookie dove in, while the Chief just sipped his beer and motioned to Netty, who was already halfway across the Brouhaha, for another round of beers.

Cochese, chewing, said, "I don't know. I don't like any of it."

"Any of what?" asked the Rookie, his mouth full.

"At this moment?" Cochese scooted back a few inches. "Your bad-breath onion rings." Then he turned serious. "I mean, I still think we're being set up. The deal happening before we got there. Wallace's lawyer waiting for him. The Egg Man not talking. He should have been our big break, but instead it's just a dead end."

Now that the Rookie and Cochese were washing down their onion rings with the last of their beers, the Chief reached for one. It was as big as a bracelet.

"Then why don't we shake him a little harder?" suggested the Chief.

"Who?"

"Jimmy James."

Netty returned with their beers. All three detectives took a big sip. Cochese was the first to speak after swallowing.

"We tried that, remember? Bobby here offered to knock his teeth down his throat."

The Rookie sheepishly took a sip of his beer.

"Then why don't we shake the tree a little harder?" asked the Chief.

"We're on thin ice as it is," replied Cochese. "If he puts in a claim of witness intimidation, he'll go scot-free. But if we handle it right, we can maybe tie him to Wallace."

The Chief grabbed another onion ring and spoke as he chewed. "Not a chance, Cochese. What do we have on him, anyway? His name showing up in the lining of Wallace's briefcase? That's circumstantial evidence at best, the same as with his car matching the one Bobby saw at the motel."

As the Chief took a big sip of beer, and the Rookie took the last of the onion rings, Cochese spoke quietly. So quietly it was hard to hear him over the sound of "Take the Money and Run" now playing on the jukebox. "Maybe we're being set up."

"What did you say, Cochese?"

"I told you before. Sabotage. Someone's fucking with us, and these are all the moves they want us to make."

"Why?" asked the Rookie.

"I don't know," answered Cochese as he tried to formulate his thoughts. "Maybe someone set up Wallace too. To get him off the street. Same with Jimmy James. Think about it. Why put the Egg Man's name in the lining of the briefcase? Who else but us would even check for something like that?"

The three detectives considered this. The Rookie spoke first.

"And who would want Wallace and James out of the way?"

"The competition, probably," answered the Chief. "Which is why we need to find out who he was in town to see."

Cochese drained the last of his beer, and when he

returned the mug to the table, he did so with force. Half the cops in the Brouhaha looked their way. He said, "Maybe you're right, Chief."

"About what?"

"About trying harder with Jimmy James."

"But he's in the lockup," said the Rookie.

Cochese shook his head. That's not what he was thinking.

"Then what's your idea?"

Cochese stood up, took a twenty out of his wallet, and dropped the bill on the table.

"The Egg Man's apartment. Let's pay it a visit."

"We did that already, remember?"

"No, I mean, *inside.*"

"Without a warrant?" Now the Chief was standing too. "If anyone catches us, it'd be our badges."

Cochese just grinned. "Well, then," he said, "let's not get caught."

As THE SUN went down, Los Angeles seemed like a different city. The heat from earlier in the day was gone and the smog had lifted. The Hollywood sign looked as white as teeth and the sky was streaked with cottony clouds stretched against a pink-purple sky. Palm trees swayed in the breeze, and you could almost smell the beach. It was hard to believe that—just a few generations ago—this place had been a desert, a ghost town. Nothing.

As he turned from Santa Monica to Highland, Cochese pointed out a liquor store.

"That was the first bust Roy and I ever made."

The Rookie, in the back seat, looked through the Plymouth's rear window at the liquor store that was getting smaller as they drove in the opposite direction.

"What happened?"

"We'd gotten the call on the radio, about the robbery. 'See the man.' You know the drill. But when we got there, the guy behind the counter said there'd been a mistake. That everything was fine."

"So which was it?"

This was the Rookie and Cochese's conversation. The Chief just sat there, wearing silver sunglasses he needed less and less by the minute.

"I thought it was a mix-up. That the dispatcher had sent us to the wrong place. But Roy *knew*." There was pride in Cochese's voice. Stopped behind the light at Melrose, he found Bobby's eyes in the rearview mirror. "Back on the sidewalk, he said that *that* was the guy. The guy behind the counter. I said that it couldn't be, but Roy told me to trust him. So I watched the front and he went around the back."

"What did he find?"

The light turned green and Cochese drove through the intersection.

"He found the owner, tied up and pistol-whipped. It turned out that the nice young man I'd been convinced was the liquor store employee was actually a double-murderer out on parole. He'd been released from the joint just that morning."

The Rookie was in awe. "How did Shadrach know?"

Cochese shrugged as he turned right, taking Oakwood through residential streets instead of bothering with Beverly at rush hour. "He just knew."

The Chief finally joined the conversation. He turned around and tapped his temple. "It's like I'm always telling you, Bobby. Check your head. It's all up there."

They parked on Hayworth, a block from the Shambala.

As nonchalantly as they could, the three of them climbed the steps toward the back of the apartment complex where Jimmy James lived. By now it was almost six o'clock. People were coming home from work or going out for the night. If somebody saw them, and called in a robbery, the detectives would have had a hard time explaining their actions. But the Chief was fast, picking the cheap lock in seconds. In a flash, they were inside.

Jimmy James's room was bathed in a white glow, thanks to the large neon lotus flower that hung outside his window. The detectives didn't even have to turn on a lamp to see.

"What are we looking for?" asked the Rookie in a whisper.

"I don't know," answered the Chief. "Anything that ties him to Wallace. Or the supplier."

"Like what?"

"A slip of paper with a phone number on it, or an address. Jesus, Bobby, figure it out."

The Rookie grumbled and grabbed a stack of mail that was sitting on a pile of old newspapers.

From across the room, as he was rifling through the couch cushions, Cochese called out, "Nothing here, Chief."

The Chief, who'd gone into the bedroom, replied, "Same here. Just some clothes and a few books."

Bobby drifted into the kitchen. He opened the refrigerator. Other than a few cans of Brass Monkey, it was empty.

"Looks like this guy wasn't the kind to plan ahead."

"Maybe he was planning on skipping town with Wallace," suggested Cochese.

The Chief reentered the room.

"I don't think so. I don't see a suitcase."

The three detectives looked around the apartment. They could hear the sound of traffic outside and, somewhere far off, a siren.

Cochese sat down on a couch in front of a glass coffee table. On the table was a jigsaw puzzle. It was mostly complete. Cochese absentmindedly picked up a few pieces and put them into place.

"What's that?" the Rookie asked, looking down at the nearly completed picture.

"London Bridge," replied the Chief, glancing quickly to the coffee table before resuming his search of the room.

Cochese put in a few more pieces before suddenly leaning forward and asking, "Hey, you think it means something?"

"Yeah, that the Egg Man was bored," replied the Chief, sarcastically. "He was probably sitting around here today with nothing to do because we nabbed Wallace before *he* could drop him off wherever he was supposed to drop him. He did the puzzle, and when he got hungry, he headed for Farmers Market. That's when we grabbed him."

Bobby got down on his knees so he could examine the puzzle more closely. It looked like any other puzzle. The picture—an old oil painting—was done in bright colors, the bridge bathed in light with boats underneath charting their paths through choppy waves.

"London Bridge. That's in England, right?"

The Chief, opening and closing cabinets in the kitchen, called out, "Good work, Bobby. You figure that out all by yourself?"

But the Rookie ignored him. He said, "Wallace is English. Maybe he gave it to James, and it's some sort of code."

"But for what?" Cochese asked.

The Rookie shook his head. He didn't have an answer.

Across the room, the Chief was unscrewing the mouthpiece of the Egg Man's telephone.

"Looking for bugs," explained the Chief. "I want to make sure whoever was Wallace's supplier doesn't know we're on his trail."

"Good idea," Cochese said. He got off the couch and began looking behind the paintings and photos on the walls. Bobby, joining in, got down on the floor to look underneath the coffee table.

"Guys!" he shouted. "Down here. Look!"

Cochese and the Chief dropped to the floor and joined the Rookie underneath the coffee table. They were packed like sardines in a tin.

"What is that?" asked Cochese.

As the Chief pulled out a small flashlight, Bobby answered, "Writing."

There, on the underside of the puzzle, spanning several pieces, *2:00 PM* was written in elegant script.

Now that all three detectives had seen the writing, they shimmied out from under the coffee table.

"What do you think it means?" asked Bobby.

"Maybe it's some sort of code," replied Cochese.

The Chief paced back and forth along the worn brown carpet behind the couch.

"Or maybe a message. Wallace probably gave him the puzzle in pieces, in a box. That way, even if we picked him up, we wouldn't have known what it was or what it meant."

Cochese whistled. He was impressed. "Okay," he said, "Wallace got the Egg Man a message with a time to meet up. But where?"

"London Bridge?" suggested the Rookie.

"No," answered the Chief, still pacing. "James didn't have any plane tickets on him and we didn't find anything here suggesting he was about to skip town."

Cochese leaned forward and slammed his hand against the coffee table. The force of the blow caused the pieces to separate and break apart. The puzzle was no longer a picture.

"Then we're right back where we started," he said.

The Chief stopped pacing and walked toward the coffee table.

"Not exactly." He reached down and picked up a few of the puzzle pieces. He looked at them. Water. Waves. Part of a dock. "It's all here. We just need to put it together."

BACK AT THE Brouhaha, the crowd had thinned only slightly. The booth they'd occupied earlier was now filled with four LAPD cops in uniform, all of whom were trying to get Netty's phone number. Since there was nowhere to sit, the three detectives stood at the bar. Since returning from Jimmy James's apartment, neither of them had come up with much else in terms of Wallace or Roy or the Egg Man, so they just stood there, drinking their beers and thinking.

Their thoughts were broken when an old vice cop named Dean Futterman entered the bar, wedged himself between the Chief and Cochese, and ordered a boilermaker. He downed it in three gulps, one for the whiskey and two for the beer.

"Jesus, Futterman," said the Chief. "Slow down. You just got here."

He held up a finger and announced grandly, "Futterman's Rule states that when two are served, you may begin to eat." He then ordered another boilermaker.

"Yeah," said Cochese, "but those are two drinks, not food."

Futterman grinned and said, "You have your way of doing things, and I have mine."

When the other boilermaker arrived, he downed the second one just as quick as the first. All at once his body seemed to slump. It looked like if it wasn't for the bar he was leaning on, he'd fall over right there.

Trying to make conversation, the Chief asked, "How goes things, Futterman?"

"Lousy day," he answered. "Goddamn traffic. I just drove in from downtown and the traffic on the bridge—I tell you, the traffic in this goddamn city gets worse by the—"

Cochese cut him off. "Bridge? What bridge?"

"Easy, Cochese," said the Chief. "Let the man speak."

There was silence as Futterman looked from Cochese to the Chief, the Chief to Cochese, not sure who to respond to. He finally decided on Cochese.

"What bridge do you think? The one in all the movies."

"Sixth Street," said the Rookie. "The viaduct."

"That's right," said Futterman. He was now bored with the discussion and flagged down the bartender, ordering, this time, just a beer.

"The puzzle," Cochese said, "it was a clue."

"Cochese, what are you talking about?" asked the Chief.

"In Jimmy James's apartment. The puzzle. London Bridge. It was a clue from Wallace to the Egg Man."

"About what?" asked the Rookie.

As the three detectives tried to concentrate, "That Lady" by the Isley Brothers blared out of the jukebox.

"The time, on the back," Cochese finally said.

"The Sixth Street Bridge," added the Chief. "It was to tell the Egg Man where and when to meet Wallace."

The name caught Futterman's ear. "Wallace?" he said. "Stewart Wallace?"

"Yeah," the Chief answered, somewhat defensively, "we busted him earlier today. What about him?"

"Didn't you guys hear?" Futterman asked. "Wallace is dead."

A C T

II

THE MORGUE WAS located on Mission, near where the 5 and 10 freeways intersect in enormous loops of concrete, blacktop, and steel. The low hum of the nearby traffic could be heard from every room in the building, even here, in the basement where they kept the bodies. The coroner had pulled Wallace out of one of the freezers so the three detectives could get a good look. It was a hell of a way to start the day.

Wallace, already pale, was now positively white. The color of his skin matched perfectly the sheet that was draped over his naked and lifeless body. Even his hair and mustache, canary-yellow blond, seemed to have grown paler since they all saw him in the back of their Plymouth less than twenty-four hours before.

"I can't believe it," the Rookie said. He looked at his watch, a cheap Timex. "This time yesterday I hadn't even met the guy. And now he's dead."

"People die all the time," the Chief said. He was wearing his sunglasses. Cochese and the Rookie had taken theirs off when they entered the building. "Besides, *we* didn't kill him."

Cochese went from staring at the corpse to looking at the Chief.

"Then who did?"

"I don't know." The Chief shrugged. "Could have been anyone."

The coroner, a tall and bony man named Dr. Lee, was standing at the periphery of the trio. The Chief called over to him.

"How did it happen, Doc?"

The coroner approached and pointed toward Wallace's neck.

"Strangulation. Garroted, actually. Most likely with a wire attached to two pieces of wood. You can see where it cut into the skin."

As he pointed, Cochese and the Rookie bent over to get a good look. The Chief didn't bother. Around almost the entire circumference of Wallace's neck was a deep wound. The outer edges were already purple and scabbing, but the inside was bright red. It made Wallace look like a doll with a head that could turn all the way around.

"Time of death?" asked Cochese.

"We're placing it between ten and eleven last night."

The Rookie chimed in. "Where did it happen?"

"He was found in an abandoned cab near Koreatown. Someone was out walking their dog and called it in."

"Cab?" the Chief said. "What company?"

The coroner shook his head. "It was a livery. Some old checker cab that'd been painted black. I was the one on the scene. I looked, but didn't find a taxi license or name of the driver."

Cochese added, "And I read the sheet on it when I got in this morning. They traced the registration to a guy out in Burbank. He says he sold it six months ago for cash. Placed an ad in the *Herald Examiner*. Couldn't remember the guy's name who bought it."

"Shit," said the Chief, kicking at one of the wheels of the gurney. It shifted a few inches, Wallace lurching one way and then the other. "Then we got nothing."

The Rookie circled around the body and looked at Wallace for some kind of clue. "So then, what was it?" he asked. "Robbery gone wrong?"

"But who was robbing who?" replied Cochese. "You think Wallace wanted to steal an old cab, and the driver did this in self-defense?"

"I seriously doubt that." The coroner came around the gurney and pointed to where the wound on Wallace's neck was the deepest. "The way the wire cut into his neck, right here, makes me think the assailant was sitting in the back seat. To Wallace's left. If the driver had done it, while sitting in the front seat at least, he would have had to swing around and pull Wallace toward him. If that'd been the case, the deepest wounds would have been at the back of Wallace's neck and not here, on the side."

The Chief finally approached Wallace and looked at his neck from various angles.

"Then I guess Wallace just got in the cab to go somewhere, but before they got rolling, somebody hopped in to go along for the ride. The cabbie, sensing trouble, scrammed. After all, no one wants to be the witness to a murder, especially if you're driving an unregistered and unlicensed taxi."

"Great," announced Cochese, kicking the gurney. This time, Wallace didn't move. "Then it's another goddamn dead end."

"What about the lawyer?" asked the Rookie. "Didn't he pick up Wallace yesterday? Maybe he knew where he went, or where he was going."

"Wallace left the station on his own," replied Cochese. "After making bail, the lawyer had to be in court later that day. I guess we could drive over the hill and pick him up to see if he changes his story."

"Not worth it," said the Chief. "He'd tell us even less than the Egg Man. All he has to do is cite attorney client privilege."

"Then what do we do?" asked the Rookie.

"We have the cab," suggested Cochese, "it was impounded."

"Forget the cab," said the Chief. "It won't tell us anything you didn't already read in the report. We need to find the driver."

"Why?"

"I want to know what his last words were," the Chief announced. "Maybe that'll tell us where Wallace was going."

"But the bridge," reminded the Rookie. "The puzzle. We have to be there by two."

The Chief glanced at his watch. It was silver and matched his hair, mustache, and sunglasses. It wasn't even ten. "We've got plenty of time."

"But still no Roy," said Cochese as they began to head for the exit.

Behind them, Dr. Lee wheeled Wallace back into the freezer.

BECAUSE THE DRIVER of Wallace's taxi wasn't with any of the licensed or radio-dispatched cab companies, it meant he was a free-floating gypsy. And rather than roaming the city looking for fares, livery drivers tended to congregate wherever lots of taxis were needed throughout the day. The Chief's plan was to check the bigger cab stands around town and ask a few questions. Union Station was just a short drive from the morgue, so they decided to head there first. If they didn't get a good lead, they'd try the airport and, if they had time before whatever was happening at the Sixth Street Bridge at two, the Greyhound terminal downtown.

As the three detectives parked along a red curb lined with palm trees, the clock built into the station's mission-like spire was just hitting 10:00 AM.

Union Station was built in a Spanish style, with a red-tiled roof and huge arched windows that looked into the waiting area. The big trains from up north and out east wouldn't start pulling in for another hour or so, the first being Seattle's Coast Starlight, due just before noon. Until then, it was just the smaller passenger trains pushing off a few people here and there from places like Ventura, Oxnard, and San Diego.

The line of cabs was long and lazy. The drivers swapped stories more than they picked up passengers. Windows were rolled down and a cool breeze traveled from car to car, the air fresheners dangling from the rearview mirrors making a pine-scented wind that accosted the nostrils of Johnny Ryall, the old guy who'd run the taxi stand for as long as anyone could remember. If it weren't for the mariachis tuning up down on Olvera Street, Ryall could have taken a nap.

The three detectives approached.

"Johnny!" the Chief called out. "My man!"

Ryall turned and, upon seeing the Chief, smiled wide.

"Chief! How the hell are you?"

While the two were exchanging hugs, Cochese whispered to the Rookie, "Does *everyone* call him 'Chief'?"

Johnny Ryall said, "What can I do you for, Chief?"

"I'm looking for a cab driver."

Ryall stepped back to give a clear view of all the taxis waiting for fares.

"Sorry, I'm looking for a driver *without* a cab." The Chief leaned in and spoke in a confidential tone. "Guy got iced last night near Koreatown. Was found in a cab. We figure he was jumped before the driver could take him anywhere, and when the action started, the driver took off. I'm hoping to find whoever that was and ask him some questions."

Ryall nodded. "Got it. So what do you need from me?"

"I just want to know if you'd noticed anyone missing today. You know, one of your regulars."

Ryall pushed a red hat with a black bill to the back of his head, revealing white hair sculpted into waves with Brylcreem.

"To be honest, Chief, all these spics look the same to me."

The Chief bristled at this but let it go. "No worries, Johnny," he said, pleasantly. "But could you give it a try? It'd mean a lot to me and the boys here."

Ryall scratched his head and seemed lost in thought.

Over on the platform, a conductor announced final boarding for a Fresno-bound Amtrak. Suddenly, he snapped his fingers. "Actually, now that you mention it, one of my best guys didn't show up today."

"Who's that?"

"Julio Rodriguez. He's usually the first guy here in the morning. Real nice guy. Dependable, especially for a wet-back."

Ryall laughed and then looked to the Chief, Cochese, and the Rookie, hoping they'd join in. None of them did. Chastened slightly, he continued. "I thought it was weird he didn't show up, you know? I asked one of his buddies here where he was, but he just mumbled something I couldn't really understand. My Spanish is not so hot."

"I understand, Johnny." The tone in the Chief's voice was soft and friendly, as if he were talking to a dull child. "Can you point him out to me? The friend, I mean."

"Yeah, sure. Right there." Ryall turned and pointed. "Third one in line."

The Chief nodded and left Ryall and the other detectives. They watched as he walked to the cab and tapped on the windshield. The driver emerged reluctantly. He was short and dark, and the Chief had to bend over so they could have a face-to-face conversation. They were too far away for the others to hear what was being said. Two minutes later, the Chief shook the man's hand and rejoined the others.

"What'd he say, Chief?" asked Cochese.

"Got a general location. It's in your old stomping grounds, Bobby." As they began to head back to the Plymouth, he turned to Ryall. "You have a nice day, Johnny. Thanks for your help."

Ryall wouldn't look the Chief in the eyes. Maybe because, with the sunglasses, all he'd see is himself.

"Yeah, uh, sure."

The detectives piled into Cochese's Plymouth. The Chief told them to head for Boyle Heights. On the way, the Rookie asked, "Hey, Chief. Did it bother you, Ryall saying that about spics and wetbacks?"

The Chief was silent, watching the streets go by instead of answering. He saw where the funicular used to take passengers to the top of Bunker Hill. To a poor Mexican from the Eastside, Angels Flight was Disneyland. Now it's gone, bulldozed to make way for office buildings. He finally answered. "What, you think I'm an idiot? That I don't know that there are people like Johnny Ryall in this city?" The Chief paused for a second before continuing. "My dad was in the Zoot Suit Riots, so none of that is news to me."

"Zoot Suit Riots," repeated Cochese. "What's that?"

"During the war. Forty-three. A bunch of servicemen here in Los Angeles didn't like the way the Mexicans were dressing." The Chief laughed as he spoke. As if, after all this time, he still couldn't believe it. "They felt that the outfits of my ancestors were *unpatriotic*."

"Unpatriotic how?" asked the Rookie.

"Too flashy," answered the Chief. "Too weird. Too *foreign*. So these guys decided to take the Mexicans down a few pegs."

"Meaning, what?" Cochese was stuck behind a light, so he looked over at the Chief.

"It meant murder, Cochese. Assault. Beatings. You name it."

"Jesus," the Rookie and Cochese said in unison. The light changed and Cochese turned. They were now in Boyle Heights.

"It went on for days," the Chief continued. "My dad was working at a movie theater at the time. He was only nineteen, but he'd been married to my mom for a year already. In fact, she was eight months pregnant. With me."

"What happened?"

"Bunch of drunk sailors trashed the place. They even pulled two guys in zoot suits from the audience and made them strip and then pissed on their fancy clothes. Hell, my dad got off easy with nothing but two teeth knocked out and a black eye."

"Goddamn, Chief," said the Rookie.

"You know what the funniest thing was? You know who was arrested that day? My father." The Chief slapped the dashboard, as if he had to hit something. "Fucking sailors got off scot-free. Some people even applauded them. Said they were 'doing the city a service.' But you know what?"

"What?"

"We're still here." The Chief watched the streets go by. The movie theater where his dad was attacked was just a few blocks away. As a new cop, the Chief had patrolled the area. But by then his father had been in the ground for a year. He never got to see his son wear the uniform. "Now *I'm* the guy with the badge."

"Is that why you became a cop?" asked the Rookie.

The Chief grinned and replied, *"Más o menos."*

TURNING ONTO SOTO from Wabash, they tried to figure out which of the houses Julio Rodriguez probably shared with half a dozen men like himself, each of them doing whatever kind of work they could just to send a couple of bucks back to Mexico each month. The houses were all the same. Old, broken, crumbling. The entire block needed a new coat of paint.

The three detectives parked and got out of the Plymouth.

"Chief?" said the Rookie, his voice rising. "You think this is a good idea?"

The Chief, his head ping-ponging back and forth as he looked from window to window, said simply, "You gotta do what you gotta do."

Toward the end of the block, something moved. A curtain swayed in a window.

"There." The Chief pointed. "Let's try there."

The Rookie led the way, with Cochese following. The Chief made a mental note that there was a back entrance to the house they were approaching, with a motorcycle leaning against a chain-link fence. The bike was a piece of shit, but it might come in handy if a guy wanted to get away bad enough.

At the top of the stairs, the Rookie knocked lightly on the door.

"Jesus, Bobby, you're going to have to give it more than that," scolded Cochese. "You're a cop, not the Avon lady."

The Rookie's neck turned red as he balled up his hand and pounded on the door with the heel of his fist. A few seconds later, a brown face opened the door a few inches.

"Oh, hello, sir. I'm a detective." The Rookie sounded surprised, as if he really hadn't counted on anyone opening the door. "I'm looking for Julio Rodriguez. Can you tell me, uh, does he live here?"

"No. No Julio. Goodbye."

The door slammed shut. The Rookie turned toward Cochese and the Chief.

"I guess he's not here."

The Chief approached and pushed the Rookie out of the way. Cochese did his best to hide his laughter. Now it was the Chief's turn to pound on the door.

"Abre la puerta. Sólo queremos preguntar a Julio unos questions, somos la policía."

While he was waiting for an answer, the Chief noticed the stunned looks on the faces of his fellow detectives.

"What, you didn't know I spoke Spanish?"

The face returned, but instead of saying anything, the door was opened all the way instead of just a few inches. The man, a short Mexican with deep-set features and jet-black hair combed straight back, stepped aside to let them enter. So they did.

It was dark, and the place smelled of pork and sweat. The windows were closed, and there was nothing in the apartment except old furniture and men in work shirts staring at the ground, each face sadder than the next until the one who answered the door led them to a bedroom toward the back of the house. He pointed to the saddest-looking one and said, *"Aquí, este es el hombre que busca."*

"Chief," Cochese whispered. "What's he saying?"

The Chief answered without turning around to face the detective.

"He said this is who we're looking for." The Chief took off his sunglasses. The man was sitting on the floor, his back to the wall. He was wearing dark denim pants and a white T-shirt. The room was dark, but he seemed to be a big man, as did some of the others lurking in the shadows around the apartment.

"*¿Eres Julio Rodriguez?*"

"*Sí, señor. Yo soy Julio Rodriguez.*"

The Chief's eyes were finally adjusting to the half-light of the room. He could see, tacked onto the wall, a picture of Julio posing with what looked to be his wife and four children. Three girls and a boy. The background was sand dunes and cactuses.

After the Chief and Julio talked for a few minutes, the Rookie asked, anxious, "What's he saying?"

"He picked up Wallace," responded the Chief. "He knows it was him from his hair and the accent."

The Chief turned back to Julio and asked him more questions. He wanted to know what happened in the cab, and if the driver had got a good look at whoever killed Wallace.

But Julio didn't want to answer. His dark eyes darted around the room, as if looking for an escape. But there wasn't one. So he began to talk.

As Julio spoke, slowly and quietly, the other men in the room shifted uneasily. By Cochese's count, there were six guys but only three of them. He didn't like those odds.

"Now what, Chief?" asked the Rookie. "What's he saying?"

"Someone jumped into the back seat, but he didn't get a good look at the guy's face. Claims it was dark. And once Wallace started screaming, he took off and came here."

"Yeah?" said Cochese in a snide voice. "How do we know *he* didn't do it? Maybe we should search the place."

Julio buried his face in his arms, which he'd propped up on his legs, an elbow on each knee. When he spoke, it was just a whisper. *"Yo no lo hice, señor. No lo hice. Lo juro."*

Looking back at the two detectives, the Chief said, "Knock it off, I believe him."

He turned again to Julio. *"Tengo una más question. ¿Cuáles fueron las últimas palabras del hombre con rubio pelo?"*

"¿Cómo?"

"¿A dónde iba?"

"No me dijo; el nunca tuvo la oportunidad. Solamente dijo una palabra: sabotaje."

When the Chief heard this, a chill went down his spine.

"What'd he say, Chief?" Now it was Cochese whose nerves were getting to him. His voice was beginning to shake.

"He told me that Wallace said one word, right before he was murdered." The Chief stood up and began to leave the room. "Sabotage."

BACK IN THE Plymouth, none of the guys knew what to make of what they'd just learned.

"Sabotage?" the Rookie asked. "What does that mean?"

"It's like I said," Cochese responded. "Someone's setting us up. Maybe that same person set up Wallace, too."

"But why?" asked the Chief. "And why relay that information to a cabbie?"

"Maybe he'd just figured it out," answered the Rookie. "And, I don't know, he had to tell someone."

Cochese laughed darkly.

"He should have picked someone who spoke English. Or who was a little faster with the gas pedal. He might be alive now."

As they were pondering this, a car turned the corner. It was an old Chevy, riding low to the ground with gold rims and windows tinted so dark they looked like they'd been painted black. It crawled down the street, driving slower than it had any right or need to.

"What do you say we talk about this while we drive?" suggested the Chief. "Cochese, get us out of here."

Cochese snapped into action, starting the car and pulling the Plymouth away from the curb. At a stoplight, Cochese checked his watch.

"Guys, it's not even noon. What do you say we grab a bite and then stop by Roy's?"

"You're still on that?" asked the Chief.

"Of course I am; he's my partner." Cochese sounded surprised. "He's the only reason I'm still driving you bums around."

"And here I thought it was because you liked us," said the Chief.

Cochese chuckled.

"I'm just here to see if one of these rocks you're turning over has Roy underneath."

As the light turned green, the Rookie chimed in from the back seat. "I could go for some food—I'm starving. And who knows how long we'll be stuck at the bridge?"

The Chief looked at his watch.

"I don't want a repeat of yesterday, where we show up late."

"We'll make it, don't worry." Cochese put the Plymouth into an illegal U-turn and got on the freeway.

AN HOUR AND three burgers later, they were standing outside of Roy's house in Alhambra. It was a small two-bedroom, built in the 1950s when Southern California began to explode with bedroom communities absorbing the overflow of Los Angeles. Roy's house was identical to all the others up and down the quiet suburban street, except that his was unkempt and shabby. The lawn was overgrown and the paint was faded and peeling. It must have been a vibrant orange at one time, but now it looked like a peach that'd been left in the sun too long.

"You have a key?" asked the Chief.

"Not exactly."

Cochese led them around to the back of the house. The side gate was locked, but they all scaled it with no problem. As the Rookie and the Chief stood awkwardly in front of a barbecue that looked like it hadn't been used in years, Cochese pulled out a Diners Club card from his wallet.

As Cochese used the card to unlock a bedroom window, the Chief whistled and said, "Two break-ins in two days. I'd say we're on a roll."

Cochese grunted as he fought with the lock, finally getting it on the third try. It took all his effort to open the window, and even then, it only opened halfway. The three detectives each had to shimmy their way through, the Chief barely fitting.

The inside of the house matched the outside. It was dusty, dirty, and the smell wasn't much better than Julio Rodriguez's place back in Boyle Heights. In the kitchen, the sink was full of dishes, and the bedroom floor was covered in clothes.

"Big house," said the Rookie as they began to wander around. "Filthy, but big."

"It was the only thing he kept in the divorce," explained Cochese. "Flora took the kids and most of the furniture, along with a good chunk of his money. They live up in Barstow now. But Roy got the house."

Turning a corner, the Chief saw an empty room. The wallpaper was faded tin soldiers and toy drums, colored red, white, and blue. This was Mikey's room. The Chief remembered the day Roy and Flora brought Mikey home.

The Chief could even see neat lines and dates in pencil along the doorjamb, the boy's increasing height measured over time. The slivers started on 5/24/72 and continued in increments of a few centimeters until 8/2/76. Roy and Flora got divorced that fall. The marks continued after that, only they were crooked, haphazard, and without dates, as if Roy was just guessing or working from bitter memory.

"Damn, Cochese, you may be right," called out the Rookie from another part of the house. "It doesn't look like your partner's been here for a few days, if not longer."

After they'd each looked through the entire house, and found it empty, they gathered in the living room.

"I actually hoped we'd find him here sleeping off a drunk." Cochese kicked one of the legs of Shadrach's couch, moving it an inch. The sofa was brown and ugly and its cushions were in disarray, even before Cochese kicked it. "Hitting the booze again might be better than whatever it is he got himself mixed up in."

The Chief, for the first time since Cochese approached him with the news about Shadrach maybe going AWOL, turned serious. "You called his ex-wife? Parents? No one knows where he is?"

"Yes, Chief. That's the first thing I did. They had no idea where he was, so I went and found you guys at the donut place."

"This doesn't make any sense." The Chief was shaking his head. "Roy wouldn't go underground like this. Not without a good reason."

"Then what's happening?" asked the Rookie.

The Chief began to pace the living room, back and forth, back and forth. Every other step he mumbled, "I don't know."

While the Chief was pacing, and Cochese stood there deep in thought, the Rookie saw something peeking out from the edge of the couch. It was a slip of paper with writing on it. Cochese's kicking of the couch had exposed it, along with some change, a crushed can of Schlitz, and a pizza crust.

"'Ask for Janice.'"

"Bobby, be quiet," barked the Chief. "We're trying to think."

"No, Chief, here. Look."

He picked up the small piece of paper and handed it to the Chief. Cochese immediately joined them, staring at the scrap. It was square but must have been part of a larger piece of something, since there was a jagged edge from where it'd been torn. One side was dark blue and the other was white. The paper was thick, not quite card-board but stiffer than anything you'd put into a type-writer. On the white side, the words *Ask for Janice* were written in black ink.

"Cochese, is this Shadrach's writing?"

He lifted up his sunglasses, just to be sure. "No. Not even close."

"You positive?"

"Jesus, Chief, you know how many reports I've read of his? I know his writing, and that ain't it."

The Chief held up the scrap of paper and smiled. "You know what this is?"

"What, Chief?"

"Part of a matchbook. Look"—he pointed to the per-forated edge—"this is where it was ripped."

"You sure?" Cochese grabbed the scrap from the Chief. He got excited for a second, but then it passed. "Okay, Chief, but unless you know who Janice is, this doesn't tell us anything."

The Chief tapped his temple. "Think, Cochese, think. This is our first solid lead."

"How do you figure, Chief?" asked the Rookie.

"Maybe the matchbook is from a business. Like, a restaurant or something." He pointed to the scrap. "We find the other half, and we'll have an address. And that might lead us to Roy."

Cochese finally smiled, slightly.

"Guys, the bridge." The Rookie was pointing to his Timex. "We'll be late."

IN ORDER TO keep an eye on both sides of the bridge, they had to split up. The Rookie and the Chief dropped Cochese off on the north side of the bridge, while they pulled off on the shoulder at the approach to the south side. They left Cochese with a walkie-talkie and agreed to report anything suspicious, along with having check-ins every ten minutes. After an hour, all they'd seen were hundreds of cars pass over the bridge without incident.

"Chief, I'm bored."

The Rookie was in the front seat for the first time since they left the donut shop the day before. The walkie-talkie was by his side, and in his lap was a pair of binocu-lars.

"Try and stay alert, Bobby. It's a bit past two. If any-thing's going to happen, it'll happen now."

"But who do we think's even going to show up? Wal-lace is dead and Jimmy James will be in the lockup until we spring him. Which will be soon unless we come up with something to charge him with."

"I know all that, Bobby, believe me."

"Then what are we looking for?"

"Someone had to connect Wallace and James. A local

guy like the Egg Man wouldn't have been on the radar of someone like Wallace, not in a million years. There's got to be something bigger going on."

"And you think Shadrach's tied into all of this too?"

"I didn't, until this morning. Shadrach's a good cop, and he wouldn't be laying this low without a reason. Or unless it's against his will."

The walkie-talkie crackled. "Guys, you see anything?"

The Chief nodded at the Rookie to respond. "Still nothing on our side, Cochese."

"Okay, I'll check back in another ten."

When the crackle of the walkie-talkie died down, it was replaced once again with the white noise of the cars going back and forth over the bridge. The Chief had to admit: it was a good place for a meeting. With all the traffic, there was no chance of being overheard, and because there weren't a whole lot of businesses around that part of town, no one would casually pass by.

The Chief was just about to relax his eyes a bit when he saw a truck appear at the top of the bridge. It slowed and finally stopped, hugging the curb just past the bridge's apex. There wasn't a shoulder, so cars had to drive around. Some of them honked. The Chief grabbed the walkie-talkie.

"Cochese, you seeing this?"

"The truck? Yeah, Chief. It passed right by me. Didn't get a good look at the driver, though."

"Do you think—"

The Rookie began to speak, but the Chief cut him off. "Bobby, quiet, please. Let's just see what happens."

The driver got out of the truck. The Chief traded the walkie-talkie for binoculars. He focused in on the truck driver. He was tall and tanned, wearing jeans with flares and a faded bicentennial T-shirt.

"Guy doesn't look familiar. At least not to me."

The Rookie relayed this to Cochese.

The Chief watched as the driver walked to the truck's left front tire. He bent over, inspected something, and then got back into the truck. The truck started and, a minute later, rumbled past the Rookie and the Chief.

"False alarm," the Chief said, trading the binoculars for the walkie-talkie. "Truck just passed us by, Cochese. Nothing suspicious."

"Got it, Chief."

After a few minutes of silence, in order to pass the time, the Chief spoke. "Bobby, what happened when you were in Hollenbeck Division?"

At first, the Rookie didn't answer. He just let the sound of the afternoon traffic fill the car. Finally, he responded. "What do you mean?"

"Earlier today, when we were at the cabbie's house. You couldn't wait to get out of there. Why?"

The Rookie's face reddened. He figured he'd have to have this conversation with someone at Wilshire Division sooner or later, about why he'd become a detective and put in for a transfer, but he wished it wouldn't be with a guy like the Chief.

"I really—I'd rather not talk about it."

"Bobby, come on. We're partners now." The Chief spoke softly, like he had earlier with Ryall, but this time it sounded sincere. "You can tell me anything."

"It was a four-fifteen call," Bobby began. "Didn't seem like a big deal at first. We'd responded to plenty of disturbing-the-peace calls before. My partner and I were responding as backup, just in case."

The Rookie took a deep breath before continuing. "When we got there, we saw that this was no ordinary fight between spouses. The guy was a Vietnam vet. He was drunk and had a gun. He'd already knocked his wife unconscious and shot one of the officers who'd responded. The cop was in the corner, slumped against the wall, his hat still on and bleeding everywhere. I thought he was dead, but somehow, he survived."

Bobby had to pause before telling the rest.

"The guy with the gun had gotten the drop on another cop, who'd rushed in when he heard the shots. That's what I saw when I entered the house. A woman lying on the ground, one cop covered in blood, and this crazy-ass-looking motherfucker holding a 38 Special on the other cop." Bobby banged his fist slowly against the dashboard. "And it was a guy I knew. The other cop, I mean. The one standing there. We'd been in the academy together. Had only been on the force for a few months. In fact, that night was the first real action I ever saw."

"What happened?"

It took a minute for the Rookie to answer.

"I froze. I should have pulled the trigger, right then and there. I should have dropped that dirtbag the second I entered the room. But I just, I don't know—I couldn't do it." The Rookie swallowed hard before finishing the story. "The cop tried to run for it, and when he did, the guy put two slugs into his stomach. By that time my partner had come in through the back door and saw what was happening. He put the guy down with a single shot, right through the heart."

"Jesus," said the Chief. "How was the other guy, your pal from the academy?"

"He lived. Works Juvenile Division in the Valley. We meet up at the Brouhaha occasionally for a beer." The Rookie was staring out the window as he spoke, watching the cars go by. "He says he doesn't blame me. Tells me he doesn't think he'd have been able to pull the trigger, either. But I don't know—that just seems like bullshit. Like he's trying to make me feel better. Anyway, that didn't make me too popular around the department. And it soured me on Boyle Heights. I hated driving by that house. It was right on my beat too. I passed it every goddamn day. So I just—I had to get out of uniform, and get out of there."

The Chief nodded. He was about to say something when someone walked by, the first person to do so since they'd parked there. The guy was wearing blue jeans, a black shirt, and a long black coat. He was also wearing a knitted black beanie, pulled down low over his head. As he walked, he looked from side to side. It was readily apparent to the Chief and the Rookie that he wasn't just out for a stroll.

"You think this is our guy?"

The Chief examined him. "I don't know. Could be." He reached for the walkie-talkie. "Cochese, we've got some action on our side."

The walkie-talkie came to life in a burst of static. Cochese's voice, excited, "It's about time. Give me the details."

He handed the walkie-talkie to the Rookie, who relayed the information while the Chief grabbed the binoculars and watched the man walk up the bridge. He was moving slow but purposefully, continuing to look from side to side.

"He's on the same side as you, Cochese," the Rookie was saying. "He's almost at the top of the bridge."

"I'm going to start walking. Meet him in the middle."

The Chief grabbed the walkie-talkie. "Okay, but play

it cool, Cochese. We don't know that this guy's got anything to do with Wallace or the Egg Man. You hear me?"

But the walkie-talkie was silent. Cochese had already tucked it into his back pocket and started to walk up the bridge. The guy in black was now at the top, beginning to head down the other side.

As he approached, Cochese could see that the guy had fair skin and blond hair with a mustache. He looked a lot like Wallace, and this unnerved Cochese since he'd seen Wallace on a slab in the morgue just that morning.

When Cochese and the guy were about twenty yards apart, the guy suddenly stopped, turned the other direction, and started running. Cochese took off instantly, giving chase. The man looked behind him, and seeing Cochese closing distance, ran into the road and crossed the bridge, the tails of his black coat flapping behind him. There was a gap in the cars, and as the guy sprinted across the two lanes of traffic, Cochese was right behind him.

As he hopped onto the sidewalk, the guy in black turned around, and when he did, Cochese saw he was holding a silver buck knife he proceeded to wave back and forth. Cochese began to reach for his gun, but decided against it. He figured if he could get rid of the guy's knife, it'd be a fair fight.

"Back off, motherfucker," the guy growled through clenched teeth.

Cochese tried to move closer, but when he did, the

guy lunged forward. Cochese zigzagged out of his way, only to dodge the silver blade again and again. Cochese raised his right leg in a straight line and managed to kick the knife out of the guy's hand. It went over the side of the bridge, where, a few seconds later, it landed on the concrete far below.

Back in the car, the Rookie was yelling into the walkie-talkie. "Cochese, you there? We can't see you! Tell us what's going on!"

With the knife gone, Cochese rushed forward and grabbed the guy by the throat. Panic flashed on the man's face as he backed up against the bridge's meager railing and tried to peel Cochese's fingers from his neck.

As they struggled, Cochese could feel the energy draining out of the guy's body. If he kept the hold for just a few more seconds, the guy would go limp. The guy seemed to know this, so he made one last desperate attempt to get free. He wrenched his entire body to one side in an effort to throw off Cochese. It worked, but too well. Cochese was tossed to the sidewalk, but the guy had so much momentum that he spun all the way around and, hitting the bridge's barrier at his waist, went right over the side.

THE CHIEF AND the Rookie, from their position parked on the shoulder, saw the man fall.

"Holy shit," the Chief said.

The Rookie's mouth fell open, but he was unable to make a sound.

It seemed to them as if it was happening in slow motion. The man's arms and legs were still—he wasn't flailing, as if he'd accepted his bad luck and knew what was about to happen.

If there were screams, they were drowned out by the traffic, which had once again picked up in both directions on the bridge. They didn't even hear when he landed. He just disappeared beyond the shoulder, and when he was gone, that was that. There was no trail in the sky, no reverberating sound. It was as if it never happened.

"Guys, guys." It was Cochese, who by now had jogged down to where the detectives were parked in the Plymouth. "He came at me with a knife. He went over the side as he tried to get away. I couldn't do anything to stop him."

The Chief just nodded and said, "Get in."

"Who was he?" asked the Rookie.

Cochese said he didn't know, as the Chief put the car in gear and went to where the body had landed.

They found him on a small side street that ran perpendicular to the bridge. They parked, got out, and stood over the man. One leg and an arm were bent back at unnatural angles. His long blond hair and the black knit hat covered the face that had collapsed upon impact.

"We need to find out who he is," said the Chief. "Or *was*."

When no one volunteered to go through the man's coat and pockets, the Rookie stepped forward. It was a gruesome job. The body was soft with broken bones and burst organs. The Rookie just held his breath and searched as fast as he could. No wallet. No car keys. No cash. Just a little something in the inside pocket of his jacket.

"What is it?" Cochese asked when he saw that the Rookie had found something.

"Piece of paper," the Rookie said. He unfolded it. "An address."

The Chief snatched it from his hand. It was written on a scrap of white paper.

"Fifty-nine Chrystie Street. That mean anything to you guys?"

They each shook their heads.

The Chief sighed and said, "Well, we'd better call out the meat wagon and then head back to the station. It'll take a few hours to fill out all the paperwork. We'll check out the address after that."

Cochese and the Rookie each nodded, slowly, unable to take their eyes off the man crushed against the street.

THE DETECTIVES WERE quiet as they headed to the address they'd found on the dead man. It was only six o'clock, but it'd already been a long day. The two bodies they'd seen were weighing on their minds; nobody wanted there to be a third.

The traffic was heavy, as usual. The periods where Los Angeles was free of traffic were getting more and more rare. It used to be that really late at night—or very early in the morning—you could have a small stretch of street to yourself, but not anymore. The gas crisis calmed things down for a while, but that had long passed. Now it was nothing but huge gas-guzzlers clogging the streets and filling the sky with brown air.

Occasionally you'd see one of the smaller Japanese brands—the Chief himself had a tiny red Toyota—but most people thought that those were just toys, contraptions, gizmos. Those weren't *real* cars.

Finally, as they passed Melrose, the Rookie spoke. "It wasn't your fault, Cochese. It was self-defense."

Cochese, sullen, was behind the wheel.

When he didn't respond, the Chief chimed in. "The lieutenant's behind you on this, too. You don't have a thing to worry about."

"Not a thing to worry about?" Cochese said with a

sneer. "The guy's dead, Chief. Nothing the lieutenant says is going to change that."

"He attacked you," the Rookie reminded. "He came at you with a knife."

"Yeah, after I started following him." Cochese hit the steering wheel with the heel of his left hand. They'd been over this at least five times at the station, but it still didn't sit right with him. "I just wish I knew if he was involved with Wallace. Or the Egg Man. Or finding Roy."

The Rookie called up to the front seat. "The coroner couldn't get anything off of him?"

The Chief answered. "They ran him for prints, but they didn't match anything we had on file. We'll send a copy to the Feds over the wire, but I wouldn't get your hopes up."

Cochese looked at the slip of paper they'd found on the dead man. It was sitting on top of the police radio next to the scrap they'd found at Roy's, the partial matchbook cover that said, *Ask for Janice.*

"Let's just hope this address checks out, then."

Cochese turned onto Selma from Highland. Chrystie was a few blocks down. They followed the numbers, but there was only an alley where Fifty-Nine should have been. Hollywood Boulevard, with its shining bright lights and dead-eyed tourists, was at the end of the block. They parked and got out.

Peering down the alley, they saw a doorway with a big

guy standing outside. As the three detectives approached, they could hear a loud noise that might be music coming from the open doorway. They also heard shouting, laughing, bottles being broken. Above the door, the name of the place was written in black spray paint: SABOTAGE.

They all saw it at once, but Cochese spoke first, followed quickly by the Rookie.

"Goddamnit, it's a place. *That's* what Wallace's last word meant."

"He wanted to come here. It's just—"

The Chief broke in, "Someone killed him before he could."

"And that guy on the bridge." Cochese leaned in and spoke quietly, since a group of kids strode in from the street and headed to whatever Sabotage was. The kids traded some words with the mound of flesh and muscles manning the door, and then went inside. "What did *he* have to do with this place?"

"I don't know," said the Chief, "but since we now have a connection between him and Wallace, I suggest we go in and try to find out."

The Rookie and Cochese reluctantly nodded.

They approached the guy at the door. He was wearing pants with buckles and straps all up and down the legs, as well a sleeveless white shirt that said, THE PLUGZ. His head was shaved except for a thin strip down the center, which was dyed orange and stuck straight up. A flyer stuck to the wall announced the night's entertainment: Black Flag, the Germs, Quasar.

It was $2.50 to get in. The Chief gave the guy a ten-dollar bill and told him to use the change to shave the rest of his head. The guy put the money in his mouth, chewed it, spit it out, and waved the three of them in.

It was steamy inside, even though it was a cool night. Sabotage wasn't even a club, just a sort of basement where the walls were covered in obscene graffiti, and everywhere you looked, there were weirdly dressed kids drinking and smoking and smashing against each other. The first thing the Chief saw, when his eyes adjusted to the darkness, were the words IGNORE ALIEN ORDERS written in spray paint along a wall.

"What a load of hypes and dragons," he said, trying to be heard above the racket coming from somewhere inside of Sabotage. The sound was like nothing he'd ever heard before. "I think we'd need four nark arks to clear it all out."

"I've heard about this place," said Cochese, looking around and nodding. "But I thought the fire marshals shut it down in January."

Cochese—dressed in jeans and a printed shirt, suede vest, and white satin tie—was the only one who had at least a faint chance of blending in. The Chief, in another blue suit, and the Rookie, in his polyester slacks and short-sleeve shirt, stuck out like sore thumbs. The kids, dressed in ill-fitting scraps of clothes that were covered in spray paint and held together with safety pins, eyed the detectives warily as the trio walked deeper into Sabotage's various rooms. The place was a maze, with the main hallway splitting off into nooks and crannies of different sizes. But the rooms were all the same, covered in graffiti and filled with stoned or sneering kids. Flyers on the wall advertised upcoming performances by the Weirdos, the Screamers, and the Dickies.

They finally made it all the way to the largest room. There was a band playing on a small stage set up between two pillars. There were four guys in the group, and they all had shaved heads and were wearing matching orange jumpsuits that said, on the back, QUASAR. The drummer pounded his kit like a madman while the bass player and guitarist sawed away at their instruments.

"Ain't nobody got to spell it for me!" The singer prowled the stage like a tiger as he yelled into the microphone. "Ain't nobody got to yell I can see!"

The sound coming out of the stacks of amplifiers was fast and intense. It was a loud, shocking, wall of noise.

The kids in the audience were crashing into each other and bouncing up and down like pogo sticks. It was like watching a pinball game with two dozen balls, all of them caroming and careening off each other. Some kids even hopped onto the stage and then jumped into the audience, rolling around on the heads and shoulders of the other kids before returning to the ground. The ones at the front were covered in sweat; some even had trails of blood on their faces from split lips.

"Ain't nobody got the pain I can hear!" The singer was now just screaming. "But if I have to, I'll yell in your ear!"

The three detectives winced at the assault. The Chief put his hands over his ears.

"What the hell are we looking for?" The Rookie had to shout to be heard.

"I have no idea," Cochese shouted back. "Just keep your eyes open!"

Right in front of the band, the Rookie thought he saw a face that looked familiar. He elbowed Cochese, but Cochese thought he was doing what the kids in the crowd were doing, and he just pushed his arm away.

"Cochese, the girl!" Bobby pointed. "THE GIRL."

The singer was still screaming. "Time for living! Time for giving!" But now he was jumping up and down.

The Rookie repeated what he'd just said, still pointing, but neither the Chief nor Cochese could hear him. He decided to make a move.

The Rookie ventured into the violent crowd, the song still going, the band still making their racket, the kids still bouncing and bashing into each other. Arms pushed and shoved the Rookie, slamming him into the backs of kids who pushed him right back. When he was a few feet from her, he was sure. It was Dellie, from the photo the woman had given them yesterday. The missing girl.

She looked up and their eyes met. Then her eyes got wide. She turned and began to run. The Rookie followed her as the band was finishing its song with a flurry of cymbal crashing and ferocious feedback. The crowd loved it, but seemed to show their appreciation by spitting on the band and other concertgoers.

Dellie sprinted down the main corridor, pushing kids aside as she ran. The Rookie kept his eye on her, finally turning into a small room just a few seconds after Dellie did.

The small space was filled with kids sitting on the ground. FORGET FAKE GODS was written in huge block letters that covered the whole back wall. The kids were all stoned. Some were shooting up, right out in the open, while others just slept or were passed out; it was hard to tell which. The band had started another song, but this far from the stage, the sound was dull and muted. You mainly felt it in the concrete floor, which shook from the aftershocks of the racket.

"Dellie?"

The Rookie scanned the room, but he couldn't find her face in the haze of smoke and half-light.

The Chief and Cochese finally appeared. They were out of breath.

"What is it, Bobby? What did you see?"

"The girl, that girl in the photograph." His eyes continued to scan the room as he spoke. "The one that's missing. I *saw* her."

"You're sure?" asked the Chief. "But it was so dark in there."

"Chief, I'm sure."

"Then what happened?" asked Cochese.

"She saw me and started to run." The Rookie looked at what he was wearing. He didn't look like anyone else at Sabotage, except for the Chief. "She must have known I was a cop."

Cochese said, surveying the room, "Then I guess she wants to stay missing."

A kid sitting near them lit a joint. When he did, something caught the Rookie's eye. He bent over and snatched the book of matches the kid had used. The kid looked up, figured they were cops, and let it go.

"What is it?"

The Rookie pointed to a jagged perforation on the blue matchbook. Cochese had brought the scrap they found at Roy's. He placed it on top of the matchbook the Rookie was holding. It fit perfectly.

Cochese instantly turned to the kid on the floor, the one who'd had the matchbook.

"Where'd you get this?" He picked him up and threw him against the wall. The kid's eyes opened wide. "Tell me, you rotten punk!"

The kid just stared at Cochese. He finally answered, "I just—it was sitting there."

"Where is he?" Cochese yelled, not believing what the kid had just said. "Where's Roy? TELL ME."

Cochese was yanking the kid around so much it looked like what was happening out on the main floor, where the band was still playing.

"Easy, Cochese, easy."

The Chief separated the kid from Cochese. The kid instantly slunk down to the ground and joined the rest of the dozing mass of boys and girls zonked out and leaning against the filthy, graffiti-covered walls.

"He doesn't know anything. Just let it go." Then he turned to the Rookie and grabbed the matchbook. He took one of its matches and lit it in order to read the cover's silver writing. They all spoke the words as they saw them.

"Paul's Boutique. The best in men's clothing."

Below this, in smaller type, were an address, phone number, and business hours.

"We're going there right now. Come on."

Cochese started to move, but the Chief stopped him.

"Cochese, look." The Chief pointed at the matchbook. "It's closed, okay? It's been closed for an hour. And it's all the way down in Pedro. There's no point going there now."

"That's what you say." He started again to move toward the main corridor.

"Cochese, hold on. We've already broken into two places in two days without a warrant. We do it again, and we're going to lose our badges for sure. I know you want to find Roy, but this isn't an official investigation and we need to play it cool."

"So, what, we just wait until tomorrow? Until it opens?"

"That's exactly what we do. Look, I know where the store is." The Chief pointed to the matches. "It's about ten minutes from my house. You guys pick me up in the morning and we'll go straight there. Okay?"

Cochese wasn't happy, but he accepted it. The Chief and Cochese started to leave, but the Rookie stayed right where he was.

"Bobby, let's go," said the Chief. "We got what we came for."

"The girl. Dellie," the Rookie said, slowly. He began again to scan the faces in the dark room. "We've got to help her."

"Jesus, kid, come on. Forget that. We now have our first solid lead on Wallace, not to mention Roy. There's no reason to stick around this goddamn place. Least of all, for her."

But the Rookie wouldn't budge.

"You're sure this is the room?" asked Cochese. "They all look alike."

"I'm positive. I was two steps behind her." The Rookie looked back to the main corridor just to be sure. "This is where she went."

As the three detectives stood there, unsure of their next move, a kid leaning against the back wall wearing a ripped T-shirt fell over. When he did, the detectives saw a door. They rushed for it, pushing the kid aside. It opened onto a cement staircase. They ran up the stairs, two at time. At the top, there was another door. The Rookie led the way, pushing open the door and rushing through, followed by Cochese and then the Chief.

The cool air of Hollywood Boulevard smacked them in the face. They were standing in between a porno theater and a massage parlor. Cars went lazily by in both directions. The Rookie turned back to the door they'd just come through, but it was locked. They each looked up and down the street for the girl, but there was no sign of her.

Dellie was long gone.

ACT

|||

I N THE MORNING, on the way down to San Pedro
to pick up the Chief before heading to Paul's Boutique, Cochese and the Rookie talked about the last couple of days. Sabotage and Dellie. Wallace and the guy on
the bridge. The fact that the only thing adding up was the
bodies.

That Shadrach was still missing bothered Cochese
more than it did the Rookie because Roy was Cochese's
partner. He looked upon Shadrach's disappearance as a
personal failing, like it was somehow his fault. Visiting
Roy's apartment the day before also made Cochese wonder how well he knew his partner. Shadrach had been
Cochese's hero, and with that image tarnished, it made
Cochese question everything.

The Rookie was feeling similarly lost. When he was
on duty as a cop in uniform, there were no conspiracies,
no labyrinths. Life was as black-and-white as a patrol car.
You showed up to houses that'd been robbed, or to apart-

ments where a man had smacked his wife. You rescued children in need, broke up fistfights, got drugs or hookers off the street (if only temporarily). It wasn't always safe, but it was usually simple. You knew who the bad guys were. Being a detective felt like playing sports in regular clothes. You didn't know who was who.

"It's a left here, I think." Cochese was trying to recall the directions the Chief had jotted down last night. Bobby just nodded, not even looking over. They hadn't spoken since Gardena, each lost in his own thoughts.

They turned the corner and saw a row of beat-up duplexes and apartment buildings. Between two houses, laundry was drying on the line. There was a smell in the air of fish. For the Rookie, who grew up on the East Coast, San Pedro reminded him of those little towns you'd find on the Jersey Shore, the ones that were ghost towns in the off-season. The Chief's house stood at the end of the block, beside an empty lot where two cars sat without tires, weeds where the wheels used to be.

"This is the place?" asked the Rookie.

"This is the place," confirmed Cochese.

They got out, parking the Plymouth next to the Chief's Toyota.

Cochese and Bobby began climbing the steps. Halfway up, the Chief quickly exited the house.

"Morning, guys, we all set?"

He tried to hustle them down the stairs, but the

Rookie still got a glimpse before the Chief closed the door. There was an old orange couch sagging in the middle, copies of old newspapers were everywhere, and the empty tins from TV dinners were scattered on a dining room table that, even at a distance, the Rookie could tell was cheap.

They all got into the Plymouth, the Rookie taking the back seat now that the Chief was here. As they pulled away, the Chief pointing so Cochese knew which way to go, he asked, "Any news on anything?"

"Nothing on Roy," said Cochese. "And the lieutenant's starting to ask questions."

The Chief nodded. "I was expecting that. Frankly, I'm surprised he let it go for this long. If we don't have something solid by today, we're going to have to come clean."

The Rookie chimed in from the back seat. "And nothing on the girl, either."

The Chief found Bobby's eyes in the rearview mirror.

"You should forget about her."

The Rookie just shrugged and looked out the window. All he saw were restaurants with seafood themes.

Cochese changed the subject. "Should we check with Harbor Division?"

"About what?" asked the Chief.

"We're in their backyard. If anything heavy goes down, they'd be the ones to respond. Shouldn't we at least give them a heads-up that we're here?"

The Chief just waved his hands.

"I know those boys, don't worry. If something comes up, I can handle it."

After a few more turns, they were on an old street lined with stores. The shops looked worn. Huge cranes from the docks were in the background everywhere you looked, like a shadow you could never get rid of.

"You've been in Wilshire Division for a long time, right, Chief?" the Rookie called out.

"Ever since I went through the academy in '64," the Chief answered.

"Then why do you still live down here? The commute must be a bitch."

"I grew up here. I know it." The Chief's voice was wistful. "In fact, I had my first job right over there."

He pointed out the window, to a bridge that was in the distance.

"Under the Vincent Thomas Bridge. Loading up the cruise ships with supplies. God, you should see those things. I don't know how they float, but they do."

Cochese and the Rookie chuckled.

"You were, what, a longshoreman?" Cochese asked, still laughing.

"Laugh it up, kids, but I haven't done an honest day's work since I climbed off the crane."

After another two blocks, they could see it at the end of the street: Paul's Boutique. The sign was hung at an angle on the far corner, the word PAUL'S in script with BOUTIQUE much smaller underneath. In the window were three male mannequins wearing clothes that looked trendy and expensive. Hanging on the door, the *Open for Business* sign was swinging back and forth. The Chief checked his watch: ten o'clock on the dot.

"Well, kidnappers or not, they're prompt."

Cochese drove past the store and parked in a loading zone half a block down.

"So then, what's the plan?" asked the Rookie.

The Chief thought about this for a second. "Bobby, you take the lead. You look the youngest, so I'm guessing you'll fit in more than we do."

The Rookie swallowed nervously. "So then what, I should—do I just ask for Janice?"

"Yeah, we'll all go in, look around, and see if anything looks out of the ordinary. When the time is right, ask for Janice and see what happens."

They were about to exit the car when the Chief stopped them by raising his hand.

"One more thing, be careful in there. We don't know what we're walking into, and remember, we're out of our division on unofficial business. No one knows where we are. If something bad goes down, we'll be on our own."

The Rookie and Cochese each nodded solemnly.

The Chief pointed to Cochese's shoulder holster, the brown leather against his blue short-sleeved shirt.

"Cochese, you'd better wear a jacket."

Cochese nodded, and they all got out of the car.

THE ROOKIE ENTERED first, followed by Cochese and the Chief. They immediately split up, gravitating toward different corners of the store in order to look for clues or anything out of the ordinary. But it seemed like a regular store. There was linen, silk, and cotton shirts along one wall, sweaters and imported shoes along another. Cochese stood in front of a rack of expensive-looking suits that put his own cheap clothes to shame.

"Gentlemen, may I help you?"

The voice belonged to a tall, suave black man who spoke with a Jamaican accent. He was dressed in the clothing of the store, and so looked better than any of the detectives.

The Rookie slowly stepped forward.

"Yes, uh, we'd—I mean I," he spoke in a whisper even though they were the only people in the place. "We'd like to see Janice."

There was silence for a few moments as the man looked into the eyes of each of the detectives.

"Janice?" He said the name with a slightly sinister smile. "Now, who might that be?"

The Rookie started to panic. He was reaching for his

badge when Cochese stepped forward. He said, in his friendliest southern drawl, "We were told to ask for her."

The man's grin remained, but it looked more and more pained by the second.

"And who told you to do that?"

Now it was the Chief's turn to step forward. "A friend."

The man's face finally softened.

"Yes, Janice, of course." He took a step back and pointed to a door behind where the cash register sat on a counter. "Right this way."

The man opened the door and held it open. The Rookie walked through it first, followed by Cochese. As the Chief stepped through, the man said, "The end of the hall. That is where you'll find Janice."

The Chief nodded and walked through the door. The door then closed behind them.

The hallway was long, with another door at the far end and a few open doors along the sides, two on the right and one on the left. As they walked, they saw through the open doors nothing but boxes of merchandise and racks and shelves filled with clothes.

When the Rookie reached the closed door, he didn't know whether to knock or just try the knob. He looked to Cochese and the Chief, but they both shrugged. So he tried the knob.

The door opened onto a large room that was mostly

dark. On the floor, lying on sheets of cardboard, were half a dozen women and men. It was hard to tell in the half-light, but most of them seemed to be young. They were all on their backs, heads supported with arms or jackets, their eyes mostly closed while legs and arms writhed slowly. One or two of them moaned.

The walls were cinderblock, and one window, high up on the back wall, was covered with plywood. The room had a sort of vinegary odor. The Chief saw a ray of light at the bottom of one of the walls. He figured it was a door.

A woman approached them from the shadows. She was tall, skinny, and covered in freckles. She wore a long floral dress that hung loosely on her thin body.

"Janice?" asked the Rookie in a small voice.

The woman gave a smile and led the three detectives to a corner of the room. She pointed to the ground, indicating for them to sit. They sat. She walked away, toward a small dresser near the door. She had her back to the room as she opened and closed various drawers.

"My god," whispered the Rookie, "what *is* this place?"

"Shooting gallery," replied Cochese, quietly.

"A showroom," added the Chief.

"A showroom for what?" asked the Rookie.

"For what Wallace was selling." The Chief waved to the people in the room. "Junkies get a free taste here, then they're hooked."

"But what's this got to do with Shadrach?" The

Rookie was having a hard time keeping his voice down. But no one seemed to mind. The bodies on the floor continued to squirm in a dull rhythm.

"Roy must have heard about it at Sabotage," said the Chief. "I saw plenty of hypes last night."

"Then why did he go missing?" asked Cochese, urgency in his voice.

"I don't know. But I don't think we can just start asking these junkies if they've seen your buddy, who just so happens to be a missing cop."

"So then what do we do?"

The woman was approaching. She carried a tray holding three lengths of plastic tubing and a trio of needles, each one full of a milky liquid.

The Chief whispered, "Try and fit in."

The woman placed the tray on the floor next to the Rookie. She looked like she was about to say something when a girl across the room, who'd raised herself up on her elbows, suddenly dropped to the ground again.

Janice, or whoever she was, walked over to the girl. The woman examined her and then moved to the open corridor. As she disappeared down the hallway, she called out, "We've got another one."

When the woman was gone, the Rookie looked over at the girl who'd passed out. He saw—now that his eyes had adjusted to the light—that it was Dellie. She was wearing the same clothes he'd seen her in at Sabotage the night before, except now her long brown hair was pulled back with a purple ribbon.

"Guys!" The Rookie didn't bother to lower his voice. "It's Dellie!"

The Chief and Cochese jumped up and ran to where the girl lay passed out on the ground.

"Jesus Christ, Bobby," said the Chief, "you're right."

"She overdosed," added Cochese. "Shit."

"What do we do?" The Rookie's voice was high and strained.

"We need to get her out of here."

The Chief bent down and picked up Dellie by the legs. She was as limp as a rag doll. The Rookie lifted her up from under her shoulders.

"There's a door over there, Cochese." The Chief pointed with his head since his hands were full. "Kick it open. We've got to get her to the hospital."

Cochese scanned the room and saw the light. He felt for the knob in the dark and gave it a twist, but it was locked. With two good kicks, the door came open. When the light poured into the room, none of the men and women on the floor responded. No hands moved to shield their eyes.

Once outside, the Rookie hoisted Dellie over his shoulder like a fireman. When he did so, he could feel her breath, faint and shallow, on his neck. They hustled down the alley and joined up to the street where they'd parked the Plymouth. The Chief helped Bobby get Dellie into the back seat, and then he hopped into the front.

As they pulled away from the curb, Cochese asked, "Where's the nearest hospital?"

The Chief replied, "Just get on the freeway, Cochese. We're heading back to Los Angeles."

Cochese complied, but only because he didn't think they could waste time arguing by the side of the road.

"She's dying," called out the Rookie from the back seat. "We've got to go somewhere closer. Somewhere around here."

"It's an OD, Bobby, not three bullets to the chest. As long as we get her to County General within the hour, she'll be fine. We'll call ahead. They'll be ready for us."

"But Chief, why?"

"I told you guys, we're out of our precinct and this isn't necessarily police business. We need to go somewhere in our backyard, where we have a little pull, okay? I know people at County General."

Cochese was flooring the Plymouth. At a hundred miles per hour, they were already passing where the 110 crosses the 1.

"I thought you knew people at Harbor, Chief," he said under his breath.

"Knock it off, Cochese. This is important."

From the back seat, the Rookie watched as Dellie's lips

and fingertips turned blue. He lifted her eyelids and saw pupils the size of pinheads.

"Guys, I don't like this," he shouted out. "Should I make her throw up or something?"

"No, Bobby, don't. That's dangerous." The Chief turned toward the back seat. "I know it's hard, but you just need to leave her. We'll be there in fifteen minutes, I promise."

As the Chief reached for the radio, Cochese asked, "So, who's your friend at County General?"

"Well, it's not exactly a friend," answered the Chief. "My ex-wife works there."

WHEN THEY FINALLY pulled up to the emergency room, a nurse and an orderly with a gurney were waiting for them. The Rookie jumped out of the car and ran to the other side, gently pulling out Dellie. The orderly was not so gentle. He grabbed her, picked her up, and dropped her onto the gurney. Cochese called out from the car, "I'll park and catch up with you."

The Chief nodded and they headed into the hospital.

As the orderly pushed Dellie through the hallways, the nurse—an Asian woman who didn't look much older than Dellie—went to work. She took Dellie's temperature and checked her pulse and blood pressure. In between these tasks, she asked the detectives questions, never looking up from her patient.

"How old is she?"

The Rookie was going to guess when the Chief answered, "Seventeen."

"How much does she weigh?"

This time the Chief was silent. The Rookie threw out a number.

"How much did she take? And when?"

"We don't know how much," said the Rookie. "But it was heroin. About an hour ago."

The nurse nodded and marked a few things on a chart as the orderly turned the gurney into a wider room sectioned off with spaces made out of curtains. Nurses were attending to emergencies around the room, walking quickly in and out of the various areas. The nurses' station was in the middle, with nurses conferring on charts and looking at X-rays, while another answered a phone that seemed to never stop ringing. One of the nurses, a woman about forty with light brown hair, saw the Chief and said, "You goddamn son of a bitch."

The Chief raised his hands and said, "Not now, Carol."

While Dellie was being wheeled into one of the curtained-off sections, the Chief turned to the Rookie and whispered, "You wait here."

The Rookie nodded while the Chief spoke to his ex-wife in hushed tones. She responded mostly in expletives and by hitting the Chief on the chest with enough force to send him back a few steps. The Chief pointed to the curtain, but Carol didn't want to go. He finally took her by the arm and dragged her into the enclosure where Dellie was. They stayed in there for about five minutes. When they came out, she had tears in her eyes. The Chief walked up to the Rookie, and they both sat down on some plastic chairs in the hallway.

"Everything okay?"

"Yeah," said the Chief, "she just gets emotional sometimes. It's been—I haven't seen her in a while, that's all. Anyway, the doctor's going to take a look at the girl in a few minutes."

The Rookie nodded. He then looked out to where Carol was standing behind the front desk, wiping her eyes. One of the doctors came out from behind a set of curtains, talked to Carol, and then disappeared into the space where Dellie was.

"So, how'd you two meet?"

"I met her right here." The Chief had the same wistful tone in his voice he'd had earlier that morning in San Pedro. "I was working graveyard. So was she. You bring in enough bodies at three in the morning and, well, you just get to talking, you know?"

The Rookie nodded.

"At first it made sense," the Chief continued. "She was

the only girl I'd met who worked the same crazy hours, or who saw worse stuff. When we got married, we never talked about our jobs. We didn't have to. We knew all the bad stuff each other was seeing. We understood."

After the Chief was silent a few seconds, like he didn't want to say anything else, the Rookie asked, "So, what happened?"

The Chief let out a little laugh. "I don't know. Maybe she decided she *did* want to talk about it with someone. And just because we went through the same things, that didn't mean that I was that person." He shrugged. "At least, that's what she told me later."

"I'm sorry, Chief."

He shrugged. "It happens."

The Rookie got up and looked into the room, anxious for the doctor to reappear and tell them what was going on. Then he sat back down in the chair. He finally said, softly, "They didn't even stop us."

"Who, Bobby?"

"Back at Paul's Boutique. That guy, and that woman. Janice, or whatever. When we took Dellie. They didn't even try to stop us."

The Chief shrugged again. "We did them a favor. Saves them from having to get rid of the body."

The Rookie's eyes opened wide. "They would have let her die?"

The Chief laughed and touched his temple with his

index finger. "Think, Bobby. In a business like that, there's never a shortage of customers."

The doctor came out a few minutes later. The Rookie and the Chief stood up to hear the news.

"You two gentlemen brought in the drug overdose?"

They both nodded.

"I have good news. She's going to be fine. We've got her on intravenous liquids and we're going to run some blood and urine tests. Maybe do a chest X-ray. She may also have liquid in her lungs, so we'll want to watch for pneumonia. And since she has some serious tracks on her arms, I may do a CT scan to see if there's any trauma to the brain."

"Can we talk to her?" asked the Chief. "We think she has information concerning a missing detective."

"I'm afraid she's sedated now, but she should wake up in a few hours."

After the Rookie thanked him, the doctor disappeared behind another set of curtains, his next patient waiting for him. The Chief approached the nurses' station and gave his card to the charge nurse.

"Ma'am, when the drug overdose wakes up, will you please give us a call? It's very important."

The woman tucked the card into the pocket of her white coat just as Cochese joined them.

"How's the girl?"

"She'll live, but she's sleeping right now."

He made a move to confront Dellie anyway, but the Chief stopped him.

"Cochese, she's not going to answer questions right now about Shadrach, or anything else."

He tried to shake off the Chief's grip.

"Cochese, I gave the charge nurse my card along with instructions to call us as soon as Dellie wakes up. There's nothing more we can do here."

Cochese reluctantly agreed. As they all began to head toward the exit, the Rookie said, "Chief, don't you want to say goodbye to your ex-wife?"

"I told you I thought I had friends here," the Chief said as he walked. "I was wrong."

BEFORE HEADING BACK to the station, they stopped for lunch not far from the hospital. As they were finishing their tacos, eating mostly in silence, Cochese finally spoke. "Pedro," he said.

"What about it?" asked the Chief.

"We have to go back down there."

"Why?" said the Rookie. "Paul's Boutique?"

The Chief grunted. "All we're going to find there now is a bunch of fine European clothing. There'll be no Janice, no dealer's den. At least until they're convinced the heat's died down, and that'll be a few weeks."

"Well, shit," Cochese said as he hit the table. The plastic silverware and napkins jumped a few inches. "Until sleeping beauty wakes up, we've got to do *something*. Look, we tracked Roy to San Pedro. We have to follow it up as a lead. It's the only one we've got."

The Chief just chewed.

Cochese continued. "You're from there. You've got to know where we could ask some questions. Maybe shake something loose."

"Cochese," the Chief pointed at what remained of his lunch. "Finish your food."

"Come on, Chief. Time is running out."

"Where are we going to go?" the Chief said, finally entertaining the idea. "Where would we even start?"

"How about the docks?" suggested the Rookie. "There's got to be some action down there."

"Bobby, there's forty goddamn miles of coast down there, and twenty different terminals."

"Roy mentioned something to me about Pedro once. A bar." Cochese snapped his fingers, trying to remember.

After he did this, the Chief barked at him. "There are a lot of bars in Pedro, Cochese. You're going to have to do better than that."

Finally, it came to him. "The Paul Revere," Cochese said proudly.

"That shitty little pub down the road from Fort

McArthur?" The Chief laughed. "All that place has is flat beer, ugly waitresses, and bad fish and chips."

Cochese ignored this. He said, "Shadrach told me it's where all the rough customers hang out. Maybe one of them heard something. Saw something."

The Chief just shook his head.

"Chief," Cochese continued, "it's my partner. Your ex-partner. We've got to try."

The Rookie, after swallowing the last bit of his lunch, said, "I agree with Cochese, Chief. What else are we going to do?"

"I'm telling you, it's a waste of time," the Chief tried to convince them.

But as they all got up, and into the Plymouth, the Chief knew he'd been overruled. He sulked all the way to San Pedro.

A HALF HOUR later they got off the freeway, the Chief again pointing the way. Unlike the busy docks he'd pointed out earlier, or the old shopping district where Paul's Boutique was, this area was empty. They passed block after block of dilapidated warehouses sitting at the feet of cranes rusting in the salty air.

When they pulled into the parking lot of the Paul Revere, they instantly knew the trip had been a waste. The pub looked like it'd been closed for months, if not years. The sign, featuring a painting of Paul Revere wearing a tricornered hat and hoisting a beer, was old and faded. Underneath this it said, HEY LADIES, TUESDAY IS FREE WINGS NIGHT—BRING YOUR FRIENDS. Most of the windows were boarded up, covered in graffiti. The parking lot was riddled with potholes, trash, broken glass. They pulled up next to the pub and parked. Just to stretch their legs, they all got out.

"So much for that," said the Rookie.

The Chief stood there, looking smug.

Cochese approached the building. Peering into the window, all he saw was darkness. Wiping the dirt off his hands, he walked to the center of the parking lot and scanned the area. Down the block was a set of train tracks and a loading zone next to an old warehouse. A guy wearing black overalls, a red plaid shirt, and a black knitted cap was putting boxes into the back of a truck.

"See that guy down there?"

"Sure," said the Rookie. "The guy with the boxes?"

"Come on, guys, let's go," whined the Chief. "I'm telling you, there's nothing here."

Cochese ignored this. He pointed toward the guy.

"His hat. You see that guy's hat?"

"The beanie?" said the Rookie. "What about it?"

Cochese took a few steps forward.

"The guy on the bridge. That guy who came after me. He had a hat just like that."

"Lots of guys around here have them," said the Chief. "It's cold here, I told you. Bobby, remember my jacket from the other day?"

"Yeah, but it wasn't hot yesterday," said Cochese. "Not in LA. Not on the bridge."

The Rookie pointed to the guy with the boxes.

"You think that guy has something to do with our case?"

As Cochese headed for the loading dock, he said, "There's only one way to find out."

The Chief held him back. "Goddamnit, Cochese, how many times do I have to tell you? We're on unofficial business down here. If we try and arrest this guy, there will be hell to pay with the local cops. We're in big enough trouble as it is. You hear me?"

Cochese shook him off and kept walking. The Chief reached again for his arm and grabbed it, pulling him back.

"Okay, smart-ass. You win," the Chief said with anger. "But let *me* handle this, okay?"

Cochese backed off and raised his hands in surrender.

The Chief slowly walked toward the guy, who had just picked up the last box and was on his way to loading it into the truck. The Rookie and Cochese watched from the parking lot of the Paul Revere.

When the Chief was about ten feet away, the guy saw him. At first he glanced at the Chief and was going to continue with the box. But then he did a double take, peering back at the Chief with a serious look. When the Chief got within a few feet, the guy threw the box. It knocked the Chief backward, but he managed to stay standing. He spun around, regained his footing, and gave chase.

The Rookie and Cochese saw what happened, and started running to help.

The guy in the overalls was fast, but the Chief caught up to him along a stretch of brick wall that formed part of a warehouse. There was a row of trash bags piled underneath a NO PARKING sign. The Chief leaped into the air and tackled the guy, sending them both into the garbage. As they wrestled, the guy got in two good punches to the Chief's gut, knocking the wind out of him. As the Chief doubled up in pain, he saw the guy scramble to his feet and take off, disappearing behind the warehouse.

"Chief, you okay?" the Rookie called out, running to where the Chief was now sitting up amid the bags of trash.

Without waiting for an answer, Cochese asked, "Which way did he go?"

It was still too hard to speak, his breath only slowly

coming back to him after the sprint and the blows, so the Chief just pointed.

Behind them they heard the sound of an engine starting up. The three detectives turned to see the truck the guy had been loading start to drive down the street. The guy in the overalls ran out from behind the warehouse. He quickly picked up the box that had been dropped on the ground, threw it in the back of the truck, then opened the passenger door of the moving vehicle and jumped in. The truck turned onto the street and drove past the Paul Revere. Cochese focused on the back bumper to get the license plate number, but the rectangular space was empty.

"We lost him," said the Rookie.

"And no plates," added Cochese.

The Chief had regained his breath. He stood up and said, "Well, let's check out this warehouse. Maybe it's connected somehow."

The three detectives walked around the building, but same as the pub across the street, it was vacant and looked like it had been for quite some time. Since there was no one else around to question, the three of them just stood there, the cool breeze carrying the sound of seagulls coming from the ocean, which was on the other side of the warehouse.

Finally, Cochese said, "He knew you."

The Chief scoffed at this. "Now what are you talking about, Cochese?"

"When he saw you, he knew who you were. He recognized you. Why? From where?"

"He made me for a cop, that's all. He had something to hide, and he knew I'd find it. Why else would he run?"

Cochese didn't accept this, but he didn't know what else to say, so they headed back to the parking lot.

"I'm telling you guys," said the Chief as they walked. "Pedro is a dead end. Let's go back to the station."

When neither the Rookie nor Cochese responded, he added, "Now that we know about the operation being run out of Paul's Boutique, I want to ask the Egg Man a few more questions. Maybe he can give us something else to go on."

Resigned, Cochese said, "Okay, Chief. We'll play it your way. But something's got to give. And soon."

As THEY WERE pulling into the station, they saw a familiar-looking gray Dodge sitting at the curb.

"Isn't that the Egg Man's car?" asked Bobby.

"Shit," said the Chief. "We're too late."

Cochese parked the Plymouth and they all ran inside.

At the front desk, a grinning Jimmy James was signing for his personal effects.

"Well, if it isn't the three stooges," he said as he put on his watch. "I'm a free man, boys."

The Rookie looked toward the door, and then back at the Egg Man.

"You saw my Charger? Yeah, I had a friend drop it by. I heard there'd been some bad luck with cabs lately."

"Jimmy, come on," said the Chief, trying to sound friendly, "it was just a misunderstanding. Look at it from our point of view."

"Your point of view?" James's grin disappeared and he spoke through clenched teeth. "I spent two days in a cell just because I went to Farmers Market to get some goddamn groceries. That's wrong, and you *know* it's wrong."

It was the Chief's turn to get serious. "Okay, James, if that's the way you want to play it. But we're putting the pieces of the puzzle together, and we know you're tied to Wallace."

The word *puzzle* made the Egg Man's eyes grow large, the bloodshot ovals turning into circles. But then he eased back into his shit-eating grin.

"Chief, you got nothing. You hear me? *Nothing.*" He finished taking his things out of the large brown envelope. Keys, wallet, lighter. He stuffed everything into various pockets.

Chuckling to himself, he sauntered out of the lobby and down the station's steps. The three detectives stood there, looking at each other. The Chief was about to speak—his mouth was open and he was putting a finger to his temple—when the building was rocked by a giant explosion. The whole station seemed to heave and shudder, files falling from shelves and dust and bits of plaster raining down on them from the old and now-cracked ceiling. The detectives ran outside to find a burning mass where the Egg Man's car used to be.

"Jesus Christ," said Cochese.

The Rookie started to run toward the wreckage, the name *Jimmy James* on his lips, but the Chief stopped him.

"Bobby, don't be a Boy Scout." The heat, even at this distance, was intense. "There's nothing left of him to save."

THREE HOURS LATER, there were still explosives experts looking for clues and making sure there was nothing left of the bomb. The news crews were long gone, as well as the nosy neighbors and passersby gawking at the macabre site. Various bits of the car were scattered around the small black crater near the curb, and the runoff from the fire engines slicked the street for blocks, making Venice look like a movie set.

The Rookie and Cochese were again sitting in the detectives' room, trying not to listen as the lieutenant chewed out the Chief from his office down the hall. He'd been going at it for ten minutes, berating the Chief for holding Jimmy James for two days without a charge, not to mention bringing him to the station in the first place.

"The press is going to eat us alive on this! Do you hear me?"

It must have been a rhetorical question, since the whole building could hear him.

The Chief didn't bother to defend himself, let alone mention Sabotage, Paul's Boutique, or the adventure outside of the warehouse down in San Pedro. He knew that if he couldn't connect any of that to a bust—to something concrete that the lieutenant could take to the captain—it'd all just sound like an excuse. So he kept his mouth shut.

The lieutenant's shouting was so loud that, when a phone on the desk rang in the detectives' room, the Rookie almost didn't hear it. He picked up the phone, nodded a few times, and put down the receiver.

"Who was that?" asked Cochese.

"The lab," answered the Rookie. "The report's in on the heroin we took off of Wallace. Looks like it'd been stepped on pretty badly. Was practically half baby laxative. Guy said he'd never seen—"

But before the Rookie could finish, the lieutenant stormed out of the office, slamming the door behind him. The sound rang in all of their ears. The Chief sheepishly entered the detectives' room. He sat down heavily and wiped his eyes. He looked like he'd lost a few pounds. He asked, with a grin, "Did I miss anything?"

The Rookie was about to tell him about the call from the lab when the phone rang again. This time the Chief picked it up. He listened, smiled, and quickly put it down.

"She's awake."

WHEN THE DETECTIVES arrived back at County General, they found Dellie in a room on the third floor. She was alert, sitting up in bed and sipping on orange juice. She looked a lot better than she did that morning. There were bags under her eyes, but at least they now had some life in them. Gone was the glassy stare from Sabotage, or the zonked-out zombie from Paul's Boutique. Her hair was down and the sun coming in through the window created highlights that seemed to glow.

"Good afternoon, miss," the Rookie said in a small voice. If he'd been wearing a hat, it would have been in his hand. "It's good to see you again."

She just nodded and smiled wryly, as if she usually didn't speak to the police but—since she was stuck in a hospital bed with an IV in her arm—she didn't have much choice.

"We'd just like to ask you a few questions," said the Chief, still wearing his sunglasses.

Dellie shrugged and said, "I guess I'm not going anywhere."

By now Cochese had pulled a photo of Shadrach from the files. He stepped forward and showed it to Dellie.

"Have you seen this man?"

Dellie hesitated before nodding.

"The other night. At Sabotage."

"He's missing. Do you know what happened to him?"

She answered, nervously, "They took him."

"Who?" asked Cochese. "*Who* took him?"

She let out a lungful of air before speaking, like she didn't really want to have this conversation but knew that she had to.

"There's a—there's this band. They started playing at Sabotage a few weeks ago. The Paranoids, an old hippie group from the sixties. They've got a few younger guys, but for the most part it's a bunch of old acid dropout dudes."

"What do they have to do with Roy?"

"Being in a band is sort of a cover for them."

"A cover for what?"

"Drugs. They deal to all the clubs in Southern California. They figure it's an easy way to reach their clientele. Once word spreads, kids see in the paper that they're coming to town and they head over to get their fix. They were gearing up to head out on tour. Up north, I think. That's when your friend showed up." She pointed to the photo. "They were playing Sabotage the night he was there."

"But why did they take him?"

She exhaled again before answering.

"He tracked them to Paul's Boutique. Some of the guys hang out down there; it's another way they get new customers. And, well, I guess he asked too many questions. So they grabbed him."

"When was this?" asked the Chief.

She tried to remember. "The Paranoids played on Friday night, so that would have been Saturday."

"And where is he now?"

"I don't know."

Cochese got in her face. "Don't give us that line of bullshit, sister. Tell us."

"Look, man, I'm being honest. I *don't* know."

The Chief grabbed Cochese by the shoulder and pulled him back.

Cochese, much more calm, asked, "Then who would?"

She looked around the room as if looking inside her head for a name. Finally, she produced one. "Ricky."

"Who's that?"

"Part of their crew. The band's, I mean. Like, a roadie.

The Paranoids all split town, but he stayed in LA. I saw him just yesterday."

"Do you know where can we find him?"

She shrugged. "He hangs out a lot at a health-food restaurant on Sunset called Suco de Tangerina. You might try there."

Cochese was writing all this down on his pad. "Does Ricky have a last name?"

She shook her head. "I don't know him that well. Only saw him at the club a few times. And at Paul's Boutique."

Cochese, still scribbling, asked, "Can you give us a description?"

"About five ten. Black hair, not too long."

Cochese finished writing, closed his pad. "I'm going to call this in. See if anyone else knows who this punk is. Then we'll head to Sunset and check it out for ourselves."

The Chief and the Rookie nodded. As Cochese left the room, Bobby turned to Dellie.

"You should call your mom, miss. We ran into her the other day. She's bound to be worried."

Dellie just scoffed. "That old lady's *not* my mom."

Bobby was about to say something else when the Chief cut him off. "Miss, if we need anything else, we'll contact you here. Thank you for your help." He turned to the Rookie. "Come on, Bobby."

The Rookie was turning to leave when Dellie said softly, "Wait."

The Chief hadn't heard. He was already out in the hallway.

Dellie lifted her hand. The Rookie took it.

"I just wanted to say thanks. For saving me."

Before he could respond, the Chief shouted, "Bobby!"

He just turned, and when he took his hand from hers, the Rookie discovered she'd given him a small expanse of purple ribbon. He smiled and shoved it deep into his pocket.

In the hallway, Cochese was jogging toward them. His face was white.

"Jesus, Cochese," said Bobby. "What is it?"

"We'd better find this Ricky kid. *Now.*"

"Why?" asked the Chief. "What happened?"

"A call came in to the station. On the anonymous tip line."

"Yeah, so?"

"They said they've got Roy tied to a bomb. It's going to go off at eight o'clock, and if we don't call off our investigation, they're going to kill more people."

All three detectives looked at their watches.

"Goddamn," said the Chief. "That gives us about two hours."

"What do we do?" asked the Rookie.

Cochese was already headed for the elevator. Calling behind him, he said, "We find her friend. And fast."

JUST PAST SWEETZER, they turned into the gravel lot of Suco de Tangerina. Cochese parked between a blue Fiat and a gray Alfa Romeo. An orange Datsun on the other side of the Fiat had a peace sign bumper sticker. The business next store was called Bodhisattva Vow, and in the window, it said KUNDALINI YOGA. Cochese leaped out of the Plymouth, anxious to find Ricky and get what information they could about Shadrach. The Chief had to hold him back.

"Relax, Cochese. I know that the clock is ticking, but we still need to play it cool."

"Goddamnit, Chief." He pointed at the Suco de Tangerina sign that loomed over Sunset Boulevard. The name of the restaurant was surrounded by a variety of strange symbols. "If that dipshit Ricky is in there, he's the one person who can tell us where Shadrach is. And time is running out."

"I know that, Cochese, but these are killers. We've got three bodies in three days. Remember the Egg Man? You want to end up fried, or over easy?"

Instead of an answer, Cochese just pouted and let the Chief take the lead. The Rookie trailed behind.

The dining room was small. It was just a few tables with men and women sitting alone, picking at salads, while a number of empty barstools stood in front of a low counter at the end of which was a cash register. A pass-through behind the counter exposed the kitchen, but there was no cooking or sizzling sounds, no aroma of food on a grill. Instead, the room was cool and smelled liked fruit. On the deck that overlooked the busy boulevard, three sets of couples were eating and talking. As soon as the detectives stepped inside, all the discussions stopped. Because the conversations had died down, you could hear Southside Movement's "I've Been Watching You" coming out of a small transistor radio sitting on a shelf.

A woman behind the counter, who was reading a copy of *CoEvolution Quarterly*, looked up to see what had silenced the crowd. She was wearing a big floppy hat, macramé dress, and sunglasses with round, rose-colored lenses. Her name tag read RAINBOW. The Chief pulled out one of the barstools and sat down while Cochese and the Rookie scanned the various faces for Ricky. Rainbow tossed the magazine aside, picked up a pad of paper, and approached the Chief.

"What can I get for you?" She looked over the top of her sunglasses and added, *"Officer."*

"Just give me, uh, let's see." The Chief picked up a menu. It was one page and lettered by hand, with symbols filling the margins: eyes in triangles and, at the top, a mandala in a variety of colors. The options were vegetable salads, fruit salads, and juices. The Chief turned it over, looking for sandwiches or burgers, but the other side was blank. "I'll have a celery juice," he finally said. "No, make it a lemon slush."

When she turned to get his drink, the Chief looked at Cochese. Cochese shook his head. No Ricky.

She placed the drink on the counter. "That'll be eighty cents."

The Chief tossed a dollar on top of the menu and took a sip. It needed sugar. Lots of it. When he stopped wincing, the Chief asked, "Say, is Ricky around today?"

The woman grabbed the dollar bill and stuck it into the top of her dress.

"Who wants to know?"

He noticed she wasn't wearing a bra. The Chief tried hard to concentrate. Flashing his badge, he answered, "I do."

She nodded at the pass-through behind the counter. "He helps out in the kitchen sometimes."

The Chief threw down another bill, this time a twenty. "Would he happen to be in today?"

She gave a slight nod, grabbed the cash, and then went back to both her stool and her magazine. As the Chief, the Rookie, and Cochese walked behind the counter on their way to the kitchen, Rainbow said softly, "I never liked Ricky."

In the kitchen, shelves were filled with jars and bags of honey, ground almonds, bean sprouts, alfalfa sprouts.

Along the walls were barrels of wheat germ and granola. A skinny kid wearing white sneakers, dark jeans, and a red jacket over an orange T-shirt sat on three crates that read SATICOY LEMON ASSOCIATION. He was chopping beets.

"You Ricky?"

"Sorry, this is a vegetarian restaurant." The kid didn't even bother looking up. "We don't serve pig."

Cochese began to rush him and, unlike before, the Chief didn't hold him back. The kid raised his knife, but Cochese easily knocked it out of his hand. It skidded across the floor. Cochese grabbed the kid's right hand, flipped him around, and pushed the bent arm into the small of his back. The kid grimaced in pain.

"My friend here asked you a question," Cochese said, calmly. "Are you Ricky?"

The kid nodded.

"Then why don't we take a quick ride? I'd like to ask you a few more questions."

Without waiting for an answer, Cochese led the way through a side door that emptied into the parking lot. The Chief opened the door to the Plymouth and, as Cochese got him into the car, Bobby sucker-punched Ricky in the gut.

Once inside the Plymouth, Ricky knew this wasn't a joke. As the car started up and began to pull out of the parking lot, he ran his long thin fingers over his face. The Rookie, sitting behind Cochese, was beside him.

"Where is he?" asked the Rookie.

"Where's who, man?"

"My partner," Cochese growled from the front seat, "Roy Shadrach. He disappeared a few days ago from Paul's Boutique. The Paranoids took him. You know anything about that?"

He took a right, leading the Plymouth up a winding residential street and leaving the busy traffic of Sunset Boulevard behind.

"Look, I don't know what you're talking about, okay? So just turn around and drop me off at the restaurant."

"You hang out at Sabotage, right?" asked the Chief. "You and the Paranoids?"

"Yeah, man, we hang out lots of places. What about it?"

"Cut the shit, Ricky," said Cochese. "You guys are dealing drugs to half the clubs up and down the coast. We don't care about that right now. My partner went missing a few days ago. We tracked him to Sabotage, and then Paul's Boutique. A friend of yours told us you'd know something about it."

"Look, man, I'm telling you. I *don't* know. Anyway, you cops all look the same to me."

The Rookie gave him another punch in the stomach.

"Cut the shit, you fucking punk," he yelled, "or we'll toss you out right here!"

"Okay, okay," Ricky said, his breath coming back. "Koreatown. On Oxford, near Eighth. A big old building the Paranoids took over. They've been squatting there for months."

"That's where Roy is?"

Cochese turned the car around in a cul-de-sac. They were now headed downhill, fast. Houses rushed by on either side.

"The cop? Yeah, he was snooping around Paul's Boutique a few days ago, so a few of the guys picked him up and brought him to the practice space. A few of the older dudes are a little loony. Like, acid casualties from the sixties, dig? One of them has ties to the Ecumenical Liberation Army. That's where they got the stuff for the bombs."

Ricky looked from face to face, trying to find one that was sympathetic. He came up empty.

"Look, man, it wasn't *my* idea to blast the pig. I thought just roughing him up might do the trick, but the other guys insisted. Anyway, you're too late to catch them. They just headed up to San Francisco."

The Chief glanced at his watch. He said, "We've got about forty-five minutes before the bomb goes off."

Cochese stepped on the gas.

"Thanks for the information," said the Rookie. He then opened his door. "But we're going to drop you here."

"Goddamnit, Bobby," barked the Chief, turning around. "What are you doing?"

The Rookie turned and grabbed Ricky by the shoulders. With a tremendous push, he threw him out of the car. The Chief saw the boy's panicked face as he passed by, heading for the concrete. With Cochese gunning the motor, Sunset in sight at the bottom of the hill, they didn't hear the thud as Ricky landed or any screams as they sped away.

As the Chief reached into the glove box to get the red light for the roof, he said to Bobby, "You shouldn't have done that."

But whatever Bobby replied was lost in the sound of the blaring siren as Cochese floored it through the intersection, headed for Koreatown.

"THIS IS GETTING dangerous," the Chief said to Cochese as they were barreling down Western, just a few blocks away from where the Paranoids were keeping Shadrach. The Rookie sat silently in the back, his heart still beating fast from what he'd done to Ricky just above Sunset. "If there's a bomb in a building in a residential district, this is a lot bigger than just Roy, Cochese. I've got to call for backup. We're going to need the bomb squad and a whole lot of cops to clear the area. You okay with that?"

Cochese reluctantly nodded.

The dashboard clock was showing 7:31. They had less than thirty minutes to find Roy, get him out of there, and warn everyone else about the bomb.

"Just make me a deal, Chief." When he turned violently onto West Eighth Street, and then onto Oxford, a police baton on the dash traveled quickly from one side to the other, and then back again. On the way from Hollywood to here, Cochese had only narrowly missed a dozen collisions. "Promise me we save Roy first, and worry about the bomb after."

The Chief knew that—once they got there—he wouldn't be able to stop Cochese, so he reluctantly nodded in agreement. He also knew that, if they were in the building when the bomb went off, they'd all be killed. To take his mind off this, the Chief reached into the glove box for the radio. He told dispatch where they were headed and what was waiting for them when they got there.

Now that they had turned onto Oxford, Cochese finally slowed down. All three sets of eyes were looking for the building Ricky had told them about.

Two blocks down, they saw it. It was three stories high, with lots of broken windows as well as sheets of plywood where windows used to be. On the boarded-up front door, THE PARANOIDS was written in red spray paint. Cochese ran the Plymouth onto the yellow lawn, and the three detectives jumped out. Cochese slid across the hood and, when he did, the engine was so hot it almost burned his ass.

The Chief rushed around to the side of the building, kicking open a chain-link fence. Halfway down the length of the structure, there was a door that was open.

"Guys, let's split up," said the Chief.

The Rookie and Cochese nodded in agreement.

Cochese ran around the building and found a door in the back that was locked. He gave it three kicks, and after the third, the door swung open. He entered the building and began shouting for his partner.

"Roy! Roy!"

The Rookie ran around to the other side of the building and came across another side door that was open. He entered and found a staircase. He climbed the steps all the way to the third floor. He ran up and down the halls, looking and shouting for Shadrach. Most of the rooms were empty. In a few, he saw mattresses, a random assortment of clothes, old books, and newspapers. There was nothing on the third floor, so he ran down to the second. He could hear Cochese on the floor below calling out for Roy. The Rookie checked all the rooms, yet again, there was nothing but a bit of junk here and there. No bomb. No Shadrach.

Downstairs, he ran into Cochese and the Chief. Both were out of breath.

"I can't—I can't find him—anywhere," wheezed the Chief.

"Ricky, that little fuck," said Cochese, gasping for air. "He set—he set us up. Shadrach's not—he's not here."

From behind them came a noise. They all turned to find a big black guy wearing sunglasses along with a tie and an olive-colored shirt stomping down the walkway, heading right for the detectives.

"What the fuck are you guys doing?"

The Chief pulled out his badge.

"We have reason to believe there's a bomb in this building, as well as an officer who's being restrained."

The big guy instantly backed off. "Oh, sorry. My name's Bunny, I live next door. I work the night shift as a security guard. How can I help?"

Cochese stepped forward.

"Do you know the people who live here?"

Bunny stiffened. "Those awful hippies? They never should have been here. The building had been vacant for a long time; the owner lives overseas somewhere. I was pretty happy when I saw them pack up and move out yesterday. When I heard you guys running around, I thought maybe they'd come back."

Cochese looked at the building, and then back to Bunny.

"How many people left yesterday? I'm looking for my partner. I think those people have him."

Bunny rubbed his chin. "I don't know. I didn't get a very good look at anyone." Now Bunny peered up at the building. "Did you check every room?"

The three detectives nodded, yes. Cochese looked at his watch: 7:45. Time was running out. In the distance, they could hear the sirens of approaching squad cars.

"Even the basement?"

Bunny pointed to a row of windows that were hidden by overgrown grass and weeds.

"How do we get down there?" asked Cochese.

"Should be a door around the other side," answered Bunny. "They used to keep it locked. I'd hear all kinds of things coming out of there. But I've got an ax. Let me go get it."

The three detectives ran around the building. They found the entrance to the basement just past where the Rookie had found the open side door. It was secured with a padlock on a chain. They each kicked and shoved, but nothing worked. Bunny returned with the ax and handed it to the Chief. It took three good whacks, but the lock finally came apart in a hail of sparks.

The Chief turned to Bunny. "Now go warn everyone in your building that there might be a bomb and tell them they need to get at least a block away. You got that?"

Bunny nodded, and then ran back to his building. The Rookie, Cochese, and the Chief headed into the basement.

It was dark and dank, nothing but shadows and foul smells. The Rookie found a light switch, but all it turned on was a lone bulb dangling in the middle of the room. Along the far wall, a workbench was covered with drug paraphernalia. Needles, scales, bent spoons blackened from flames.

At the end of the cavernous space was a door. Cochese ran toward it. It was locked. He kicked and shoved with his shoulder, but it wouldn't budge.

"Let me help," said the Rookie.

Together, Cochese and Bobby kicked down the door.

The room was small and covered in graffiti. Roy was along a far wall tied to a chair, and on a table in the center of the room was a round clock with black hands, white face, and gold trim. Attached to the clock, along with a bunch of wires, was enough plastic explosives to level half of Koreatown. The clock read 7:56.

"Shadrach!" called out Cochese.

Roy's mouth was sealed with a stretch of black tape. But even after Cochese ripped off the tape, Shadrach still didn't say anything. He was pale, gaunt, and looked like he could pass out any second.

The Rookie quickly untied Shadrach's hands, and Cochese helped Roy out of the basement. The Chief ran ahead. Where the Plymouth was parked, there was now an ambulance. Just as the drivers were getting out, the Chief pointed toward where Cochese and Shadrach, limping but sporting a small smile, were emerging from the side of the building. Squad cars began arriving with sirens blaring, along with a big black van that belonged to the bomb squad.

"It's in there," the Chief shouted as he pointed to the basement. "You've got about three minutes, so hurry!"

The bomb squad guys disappeared as Cochese hoisted Roy onto a stretcher and then looked to the Chief for orders about what to do next.

"Bobby, Cochese, follow me!" From the trunk he grabbed binoculars and a walkie-talkie. He barked at Cochese to grab the megaphone. Now that Roy was safe, they had to warn everyone else.

The Chief ran to the back of the building, scrambled up a toolshed and, from there, hoisted himself up to the roof. He called down for the megaphone.

"Throw it up."

The Rookie jumped onto the shed. Cochese tossed the megaphone to the Rookie, who then tossed it to the Chief. The Chief ran across three rooftops, looking for the best vantage point and the highest ground. Then he shouted into the megaphone.

"PLEASE EVACUATE YOUR HOMES. WE HAVE REASON TO BELIEVE THERE'S A BOMB IN THE AREA."

He jumped across two more rooftops and repeated the same message. The Rookie joined him and handed him the binoculars. The Rookie then ran to another building and told people to flee. Cochese, a bit in shock from finding his partner in such bad shape, merely climbed to the top of a building and surveyed the surreal scene unfolding below.

The surrounding streets were a cacophony of sirens and flashing lights. Squad cars kept showing up, along with two fire trucks and a news van. People were streaming out of their houses, the ambulance Roy was in having to briefly fight with the crowd to drive away. The sound of confused shouts mixed with the noise of everything else. It was chaos.

The Chief checked his watch. Eight o'clock. He steeled himself for the blast, but all he heard was more sirens. The Rookie was still shouting at people to get as far from the building as they could. There was the continued general cry as people ran for their lives, but no explosion.

Farther away, out toward the coast, the Chief could see the sun going down. A breeze blowing east to west stretched acres of puffy clouds across the purple sky as sunset came slowly to Los Angeles. He checked his watch again: 8:02.

The Chief breathed a sigh of relief, his body almost buckling as he exhaled. The end wasn't going to come. Not tonight, anyway.

ACT
IV

B Y THE TIME the Chief and the Rookie made it back to the station, it was almost ten. The only sign from the explosion earlier in the day was the black spot on the street and the yellow police tape marking off where Jimmy James, and his car, once stood. Cochese had caught a ride to the hospital to check on Shadrach, so they were in his car, the Rookie driving for the first time since before the Wallace bust on Monday.

The Rookie parked Cochese's Plymouth next to theirs, putting the keys above the visor. As they got out of the car, they both stretched and yawned. It had been a long couple of days, and their bodies were beginning to feel the effect. Both of them wanted nothing more than to take a hot bath and sleep for a week.

The Chief took his pistol out of his shoulder holster and gave it to the Rookie. "Stick this in our trunk until tomorrow, will you?"

The Rookie took the pistol, a four-inch Colt. He then

slipped his own six-inch Smith out of its holster. He popped the trunk and put both guns inside, nestling them inside a first aid kit. Sitting on the spare tire, he saw the Chief's trench coat from the other day. Since there was a cool breeze, the day's heat totally gone, he reached for it.

"Your jacket," said the Rookie. "You need it?"

"Nah, just leave it. I'll stay with a friend in the city tonight." He tossed the keys to the Rookie. "Hang on to these until the morning, okay?"

"Sure," the Rookie answered.

Putting the keys into his pocket, he felt the ribbon that Dellie had given him at the hospital. He thought back to the other day, after they'd left the donut shop. The woman on the street.

"The girl." He spoke slowly, as if in a dream. "Dellie."

The Chief scowled. "What about her?"

"You said that old lady wasn't her mother. She was just a foster parent. How did you know that?"

The Chief replied, annoyed, "Now what are you talking about?"

"The old lady, Chief. The one that flagged us down. She's not Dellie's biological mother. You were right. How did you know that?"

"I don't know, Bobby, it just seemed—"

"How did you know she wasn't that woman's daughter? Tell me."

The Chief was shaking his head. He didn't want to answer, but had the feeling the Rookie wasn't going to let it go.

"Because I was married to Dellie's mother, okay? She's my daughter."

The news was like a shock wave. It made the Rookie take a step back.

"The nurse, Carol. My ex-wife. That's Dellie's mom."

"Okay," the Rookie said cautiously, "you guys had Dellie. Then what happened?"

"She was taken from us, that's what happened."

"Why, Chief?"

"It was bullshit. An accident, really."

"What, Chief? *What* was an accident?"

The Chief paused for a few seconds. "She got—she was hurt. Right before her third birthday. It was a Sunday and Carol was making tea. I was supposed to be watching Dellie." Tears welled up in the Chief's eyes. "She was just trying to be helpful."

He wiped the tears away and continued speaking.

"The kettle burned her arm and the county investigated. When they did, they found other marks on Dellie, but that was bullshit too. All I ever did was spank her a little, just to keep her in line. It was Carol's fault. She was never around, so I had to handle all the discipline." The Chief slapped his hand against the hood of the Plymouth. "They told us it was just temporary, that we'd get her back. But we never did. Carol always blamed me."

The Chief stopped, as if that was all he was prepared to say. But Bobby wasn't satisfied with only having half the story.

"Keep going, Chief."

"I tracked her down. About six years ago. Dellie, I mean. I never even told Carol I was doing it. I did it on my own because I wanted to make sure she was okay. That she was being taken care of."

"How did you track her down?"

The Chief was reluctant to speak. When he finally did, he spoke fast, as if by getting the words out quickly they wouldn't be heard. "I made a contact at the Department of Children and Family Services and got access to her file. For a few years I got slipped Dellie's address and the names of her foster parents. And then I just—I'd drive by the house or something. Make sure Dellie was okay. But then my contact got fired, so I would go in there on my own. By then I knew how the department worked and how to get in and out undetected."

"But why didn't you say anything before? When the woman stopped us?"

"I couldn't, Bobby. Getting access to those records is a big deal and, well, I'd been caught before. Last summer a janitor walked in on me when I was there. I managed to get off with a slap on the wrist, but if it came up again that I'd been snooping around, I'd be bounced out of the department for sure. And then what good could I have done for her? For anyone? That's why I didn't say anything."

The Rookie kept shaking his head. The facts were all up in the air, and he was hoping they'd land in some sort of order that made sense.

"Shadrach."

"What about Roy?"

"He was part of this too, wasn't he?"

"He was doing me a favor." The Chief stopped speaking and looked around the parking lot for an escape. There wasn't one, so he kept going. "Last week, I asked him to look for Dellie. But I didn't know it would lead him to Sabotage. If I had, I'd never have put him on it."

"But why put him on it at all?"

"I told you, I'd gotten in trouble for dipping into her records, not to mention what happened all those years ago. I couldn't just drop by Dellie's house and start asking questions. So I asked Roy to make sure she was okay. That address was the last one I had."

"That's why the woman flagged us down." The Rookie leaned against the Plymouth. It was practically identical to Cochese and Roy's. "She thought we were Shadrach. That's what she meant when she said she'd talked to the police."

"I hadn't seen Dellie around for a while, so I asked Roy

to do me a favor. How he connected her to Sabotage, I don't know."

"But why didn't you tell anyone about this?"

"For Roy's sake. And mine. What he was doing, what I'd *asked* him to do, would not have been looked upon kindly by the lieutenant. We both knew that. I was trying keep him out of hot water."

"And you ended up getting him boiled in it."

"Easy, Bobby, come on."

The Chief approached the Rookie, tried to put his arm around him. But Bobby just ducked.

"Look, it all went a bit wrong. I admit that," said the Chief, "and I'm not saying it was fun, but Roy's fine now. We'll shut down Paul's Boutique, and we'll bust the Paranoids. It's a happy ending."

"Happy ending," repeated Bobby, but he didn't really believe it.

"I'm sorry I didn't tell you about it. I wanted to, really."

The Chief's voice was thick with fake sincerity. Bobby didn't buy it. When a cool breeze blew by, the smell left by the explosion was still in the air.

"Come on, let's go inside," said the Chief. "I'll buy you a cup of coffee."

Coffee was the last thing that Bobby wanted, but he followed the Chief into the building anyway.

THE LIGHTS WERE off in the detectives' room. The whole floor was empty and quiet. The bellboy uniform and chef's hat from the other day were on a filing cabinet along the wall, sitting on top.

In the corner was a two-burner hot plate that held a couple of coffeepots. Next to this were three tall stacks of Styrofoam cups and a blue mug that held stirring sticks and individual portions of cream and sugar. A tray was filled with quarters, dimes, and nickels. Someone from the building came by every couple of hours to make sure the pots were hot and full. It worked on the honor system, which you'd hope wouldn't be a problem in a building full of cops. The Chief threw down some coins and handed the Rookie a Styrofoam cup. They each grabbed a pot, poured, and left it black.

The Rookie was calm now. All of the anger and confusion from the parking lot was gone. But there were still aspects of the last couple of days that bothered him.

"Chief, something's still not making sense."

"What is it now, Bobby?"

The Chief took a sip and smarted at the taste. It must have been sitting there for hours.

"Wallace. And the Egg Man. Who killed them?"

The Chief put his coffee onto one of the desks.

"Can we do this tomorrow, Bobby?"

"No, Chief. Let's do this now."

"Look," said the Chief, exasperated, "the Egg Man was known all over town as a hood. Plenty of people probably wanted him out of the way. And Wallace, well, he just pissed off the wrong people."

The Rookie shrugged. It seemed to make sense. He yawned and was about to turn to leave when the Chief added, "That's what happens when you start stepping on your stuff."

The Rookie felt a flash of heat go through his body. "Say that again."

The Chief looked puzzled, but played along anyway. "Wallace was stepping on his stuff."

"How do you know that?"

"Know what?"

"That Wallace cut the heroin with something else."

"Did he?"

"Yes, Chief, he did. But how did you know that? It's not Wallace's MO; I read the sheet on him. He's known for buying and dealing high-quality stuff. Pharmaceutical grade. But not this time."

The Chief began to lift a finger to tap against his head, but thought against it and remained silent. So the Rookie continued. "I got a call from the lab today while you were in with the lieutenant, but I never had a chance to tell you about the report. About Wallace cutting the heroin, I mean. So I'm asking you, how do you *know* that?"

The Chief waved his hands in the air as if making some point but, without the words to go with the movement, the gesture was meaningless. When he didn't say anything, the Rookie spoke for him. "You knew it was cut because you're the one who sold it to him pure." The Rookie let this hang in the air for a second before adding, "Isn't that right, Chief?"

All he said in response was, "You're in way over your head, Bobby. You need to think carefully about what you do next. You hear me?"

Bobby put down the untouched coffee. He tried to remember back to the other day.

"You said you'd gotten the tip about the bust from an informant. Some guy you were running off book. But that's bullshit, isn't it? You didn't need an informant because you did the deal yourself. *You* were the one who set it up."

The Chief was silent, so Bobby kept going.

"You did the deal earlier that morning. You met with Wallace in our room, and then came to the station. We met Cochese at the donut shop and you asked him along, just so he'd stop asking questions about Shadrach. Only you didn't figure on Wallace sticking around, did you? He got another room. The one I saw him coming out of. You probably told him to scram in the morning, but he hung around. That was his mistake."

The Chief began biting his nails.

"And when we got the briefcase, you could tell just by looking at the heroin, couldn't you? It was more than what you'd sold him. So you knew he'd cut it with something else."

"Bobby, you're crazy."

"Am I, Chief? We can brush the room we were in. The one *you* paid for. We'll find Wallace's fingerprints. That'll be enough to prove—"

"It won't prove jack shit, Bobby, so drop it."

"Then in your house, your car, we'll find the cash, Chief. That'll connect you."

"You're wrong, Bobby, I'm telling you. You're wrong."

"Then tell me the truth, Chief. For once."

Before answering, the Chief looked to the hallway, to make sure no one was passing by. "Maybe I *was* running a little something on the side, okay? Again, it was for Dellie. She's going to be eighteen in a few months, and those assholes she's with are going to cut her loose. You think foster parents care about college? Dellie's going to be out there on her own. I was just trying to help."

"How, by running drugs?"

The Chief rushed the Rookie and made a motion for him to keep his voice down.

"Damnit, Bobby, I never sold anything. I just turned a blind eye, that's all."

"How? To who?"

Again the Chief hesitated before answering, as if he

could just wait Bobby out. "Some guys down in Pedro, okay? Who I knew from my days on the dock. I ran into them a few years ago and they talked me into it. It was all their idea."

Suddenly, Bobby flashed back to the guy near the Paul Revere, the one with the boxes.

"At the warehouse today. He was one of them, right? One of your guys? He got spooked seeing you with us, so he ran. Right? That's why you didn't want to go down there."

The Chief didn't try to deny it.

"My god, Chief, how do you live with yourself? You're supposed to be a cop."

"The stuff never came up to Wilshire Division, okay? It stayed down south or went out east. The other day, with Wallace, that was the first time it was ever in my own backyard. And it's going to be the last time, I promise."

Bobby tried to arrange the facts in his head, but they were coming at him so fast. Names, events, bodies. It all began to blur together.

"So then, what? Wallace was double-crossing you somehow, and that's why you killed him?"

"Jesus Christ, Bobby, keep your voice down. I didn't kill Wallace. How could I have? I was with you and Cochese all day. We heard it from Futterman when we were already at the Brouhaha."

"Then one of your buddies from Pedro did it. You set it all up so you could—"

"Look, it was Ricky's crew, okay?" The Chief cut him off. "They're going around town trying to wipe out the competition. First Wallace, and then the Egg Man."

"Who was that on the bridge?"

"Bridge?" the Chief snapped. Bobby was getting under his skin. "What bridge?"

"The bridge, Chief. Yesterday. The guy who attacked Cochese. Who *was* that?"

"Wallace's brother," the Chief finally answered, mumbling. "He must have thought Cochese was one of Ricky's crew. That's why he went after him. He'd never had made Cochese as a cop otherwise. He was too stupid."

"Why was the Egg Man meeting with Wallace's brother?"

"It was the drop. Wallace made the buy, and he was going to give the drugs to Jimmy James to give to his brother. This time Wallace wasn't going to take the drugs with him. His brother's the guy on the street here in LA for distribution. But we picked up Wallace and the Egg Man before that could happen. I don't know why Wallace's brother didn't get the message."

While Bobby was trying to sort the facts in his head, the Chief continued. "Look, Bobby, I know it was wrong. That's why I was getting out. Wallace was going to be the last score I helped those guys with, I swear. Because

I—it wasn't just Ricky's crew. It was . . ." The Chief's voice trailed off. He inhaled and found the energy to continue. "It was Cochese and Roy. They were hot on the trail of the Paranoids; that's the case they were working last week. That meant they were getting close to me too. To my connections in Pedro. Roy was sniffing around what I had going on, and I knew if he picked up those boys, they'd give me up in a heartbeat. I just needed to keep him busy for a couple of days while I covered my tracks."

"So you put Shadrach onto Dellie just to get him out of the way?" Bobby's head was swirling. "Goddamnit, Chief. Do you know how bad this is?"

"It was for Dellie. It was all for Dellie," he pleaded. "It's just—I wanted her to have a good life. College. I—I've saved twenty grand."

"Chief, Dellie's a junkie. She's not going to school. She's going to go to jail one of these days, and you know it."

"She could have a future. That's what I wanted to give her. That's why I did all of this. You saw my apartment today. You saw how I live. I didn't do it for myself. It was for Dellie."

"But when Roy's back," Bobby shook his head as he spoke. "Surely he'll put all this together."

The Chief laughed, the old confidence returning.

"I don't think so. If Roy tries to make any trouble, I'll

just fill him in on all the illegal activity Cochese had been up to this week. Not to mention *you*, Bobby."

"Me?" said the Rookie.

"What, have you forgotten already? You threw a man out of a moving car today. I was there. Hell, even Cochese would have to testify against you."

Bobby took a step back. It felt like someone had punched him in the stomach.

"I'm not saying I'd be the most popular guy in the department," continued the Chief, his voice drenched with sarcasm, "but you'll all keep your mouths shut if you know what's good for you."

Bobby turned his back and walked slowly to one of the filing cabinets lining the room. He remembered Cochese saying at the donut shop that Roy had left his revolver in the detectives' room. The Rookie opened the cabinet and found the gun. When he turned around, he was pointing it at the Chief.

"You're wrong, Chief. You're coming with me."

"And where would we be going, Bobby?"

"Downstairs. You're going to wait in a cell while I tell all of this to the watch commander."

The Chief laughed again.

"I'm not kidding. If you don't come with me, I'll shoot." Bobby tried to sound forceful, but it took effort. The gun shook slightly in his hands. "It's better to be judged by twelve than carried by six, so let's go."

"Bobby, fuck you. You're a pushover. I know it and you know it. Everyone at Hollenbeck knows it. Think, think." He tapped his temple. "Did you ever wonder how you ended up as my partner? I *requested* you. I heard what happened with your old partner and the Vietnam vet. I knew in your heart you were a station queen, but I figured that could come in handy one day. And when the time came, like now, you wouldn't be able to stop me from doing a goddamn thing. And I was right. You froze then, and you're going to freeze now."

"You're wrong, Chief. You're coming with me. We're going to go downstairs and I'm going to call the lieutenant and tell him what's been happening. With your record, and your years on the force, you're going to get off easy."

"I'd lose my pension. I'd lose the money." A bit of sadness crept into the Chief's voice. The grin was still there, but it was disappearing fast. "Dellie would get nothing. I can't be on the inside."

"You can do it. We'll visit you. I'll visit you."

The Chief shook his head. "Bobby, Bobby, Bobby, I hate to break it to you, but your crystal ball ain't so crystal clear. They'd throw the book at me, and if you don't think that, then you're dumber than I think you are."

"It's the only solution."

A thought seemed to occur to the Chief. "Bobby, listen. I just told you, I've got twenty grand back at my place. Let's split it. You get ten grand and I disappear for a while. Mexico, maybe. And by the time I come back, everything will be different. Okay?"

Bobby just shook his head.

The Chief looked to the hallway, and then to Bobby. The Chief began to slowly edge his way toward the door.

"Chief, stop. I'm warning you."

"You couldn't pull the trigger then, Bobby." The Chief was walking slowly toward the hallway. "And you won't be able to pull the trigger now."

"Wanna bet?"

The Rookie fired.

EPILOG

T HE DONUT SHOP, the same as every other morning, was crowded with cops. Tadlock was holding court with a quartet of young boys in uniform, brush cuts who'd only been on the force a few weeks. He shadow-boxed as he told jokes and stories of his glory days, the laughter reaching all the way to the parking lot where Bobby, Cochese, and Shadrach stood eating donuts out of a white bag that sat on the trunk of the Plymouth. The donuts didn't taste as good as they did the other day.

Shadrach's cheeks were sallow and he had bags under his eyes, as well as a bruise on his left cheek from when they'd gotten the drop on him at Paul's Boutique. He had to lean on the car for support as he sipped his coffee. When he arrived at the station for his shift, everyone told him he should have taken the rest of the week off, but he insisted on hitting the streets.

Tadlock came out with more coffee. After handing

everyone a new cup, he looked around and asked, "No Chief?"

Bobby looked to Cochese and Shadrach before turning to Tadlock and repeating, solemnly, "No Chief."

Tadlock just shrugged and went back inside. Once he was gone, Cochese asked, "Any idea where he might go?"

"He told me he had twenty grand stashed away," Bobby said. "That could take him pretty far."

"Not if he's injured," Shadrach said, "especially if it's bad."

Bobby thought back to the night before. The Chief tried to escape by darting through the door, so the bullet had caught him in the shoulder as he turned. There was a burst of blood and fabric, the Chief yelling in pain and raising a hand to the wound. Bobby had stood there for a moment, in shock. By the time he regained his senses, and walked into the hallway, the Chief was gone. There was a small bit of blood on the ground, but that was it. Downstairs, the cop on duty hadn't even seen the Chief leave.

"We can try the hospitals," said Shadrach. "Depending on how bad the wound was, he might have gone to one of them last night to get patched up."

"His ex-wife's a nurse at County General," said Bobby.

"Carol, yes," said Shadrach, "I remember her. Tough as a pistol."

"She seemed pretty pissed at him," Bobby continued.

"But that doesn't mean she wouldn't do it out of loyalty, especially if the Chief promised it would be the last time she'd ever see him."

Shadrach nodded.

Plus, there's the girl, thought Bobby. *He might have wanted to say goodbye to Dellie.*

"Then that's where we'll start." Shadrach finished one donut and started into another. "The lieutenant gave us forty-eight hours to bring him in. Otherwise, he's going to turn this over to internal affairs. So we have to act fast."

Shadrach had convinced the lieutenant it'd be better if the whole thing could be handled quietly. No stories in the *Los Angeles Times*, nothing on TV. No scandal. Gates, the new police chief, had been on duty less than a year, and no one wanted to bring that kind of publicity to the department. But once IAD got hold of it, it'd turn polit- ical. Old scores would be settled, information would be leaked, people would talk. It'd be on the front page for weeks.

"You know, it's funny." Shadrach gave a small laugh. "I haven't ridden three in a car since Watts in '65."

"You were in the riots?" asked Cochese.

Roy nodded. "Yup, along with the Chief. He was a good man. Saved my ass many times, including that night. Look, I don't know what made him go dirty, but let's try not to judge him before we have all the facts."

Cochese nodded, but Bobby didn't. He realized he'd

been holding a donut for ten minutes without taking a bite. He tossed it back into the bag. He wasn't hungry.

Shadrach and Cochese finished their donuts. As Shadrach was wiping the powdered sugar from his hands, he said, "We've been through the fire, boys, but it's about to get even hotter. We're going after one of our own. You ready?"

They both nodded.

Shadrach took the white bag and crumpled it up, tossing it into a dumpster. Bobby got into the back seat, and Cochese slid into the passenger's seat beside his partner. Shadrach started up the Plymouth.

Revving the engine, he said, "Let's go get him."

CPSIA information can be obtained
at www.ICGtesting.com
Printed in the USA
FSHW022050171119
64213FS